starting over

ALSO BY BARBIE BOHRMAN

Promise Me
Playing It Safe

BARBIE BOHRMAN

starting over

Montlake
Romance

Published by Montlake Romance, Seattle

www.apub.com

Amazon, the Amazon logo, and Montlake Romance are trademarks of Amazon.com, Inc., or its affiliates.

ISBN-13: 9781503952065
ISBN-10: 1503952061

Cover design by Eileen Carey

Printed in the United States of America

To Kyle,

Thank God for you and for Match.com.
And nope, no scenes with a hot dog cart in this one either.

Love you, always, B.

CHAPTER ONE

My daughter, Josie, is a force to be reckoned with.

I love that about her on most days. Right about now, not so much.

She's currently doing God knows what in her bedroom, completely ignoring me after I've called her twice already.

I was her age once upon a time. That glorious time in a little girl's life when you're at the precipice of puberty and really, really cranky. Ah, yes, the good ol' days of being twelve years old and not having a care in the world. They have a name for it nowadays: tween.

Back when I was a tween, I didn't want to have to answer my parents, do my homework, chores, or anything for that matter other than gab to my girlfriends and obsess over which Taylor was the hottest from Duran Duran.

For the record, it was and will always be John Taylor.

Somehow, One Direction doesn't quite cut it. But according to Josie, they are the be-all and end-all. And if I even attempt to voice any opinion to the contrary, she begins to spout off how they are the greatest band that ever lived. I don't have the heart to tell her how wrong she is. Then again, I bet that's how my mom probably felt about my obsession with Duran Duran. So I leave Josie alone about it for the most part. Some days though, I can't help but poke fun at her musical tastes.

"Josie!" I yell out one more time in the hopes she'll answer and I won't have to go investigate.

"I'm coming, Mom!"

"That wasn't so hard, was it?" I mumble under my breath.

Josie arrives like a bat out of hell in front of me. One chunk of her usually long and beautiful dirty-blonde hair is hanging limply in a very sad looking ponytail in a shocking fuchsia color. The rest of her hair is haphazardly pulled up into a hair clip. She's holding a comb in one hand and some kind of hair product bottle in the other. Her bright blue eyes are wide as if she's not sure of what's about to happen next.

Ever so calmly, I ask, "That washes out, right?"

"Oh, this?" Her eyes dart up until I mostly see the whites of her eyes. "Yeah, it washes out. I just wanted to see if I could rock the pink."

"Rock the pink?"

"*Moooom*, my gosh! Yes, you know, rock the pink look in my hair."

I bite my lip to keep from laughing. One, because I used to say "mom" just like that to my own mother. Two, because her hair looks ridiculous and I hope she didn't intend to walk out of this house looking like that. And three, because she's so exasperated about having to explain what "rock the pink" means to me, because she thinks I'm so out of touch with what's cool and hip.

"Are you planning on washing it out before or after dinner?" I ask.

"How much time do I have?"

I glance over to the taco meat bubbling nicely on the stovetop. "I'd say you have about ten minutes, tops."

"After dinner then."

She turns on her heel to head back toward her bedroom, but then she stops and asks, "Do you need any help?"

Now there is the baby girl I know and love. I smile brightly and say, "I would love it if you helped."

Josie puts down the comb and hair-color spray bottle on the kitchen island and proceeds to get all the serving dishes ready for our Tuesday Taco Night, which has been a tradition of ours since she was five years old. Back when she was the pickiest eater on the face of the earth. Back when her whole life consisted of Elmo, learning her ABCs, and snuggling up with me so I could read her a chapter from one of the Harry Potter books. Back when she would jump into my bed on a Sunday morning and we would lazily goof around until it was time for lunch, bypassing breakfast altogether.

As Josie gets older, each year goes by faster and faster. It's as if the time that was once so precious is disappearing right from under my nose if I blink for even a second too long. As she sets the table, I'm reminded of how she changes with each passing day. I see it in every little thing she does. Like the way her face scrunches up lately when she takes a bite of food that she doesn't like. The way her legs get longer and longer until the day will inevitably come that she'll be as tall or even taller than me. The way her cheeks that I so loved to give big, wet kisses to for no reason in particular have lost all of their baby fat.

It's official. I don't want my baby to grow up.

Josie's been my partner in crime since the day she came into this world. It's always been us against the world. And I will always put her first before anything or anybody, including myself. Which is how every parent should be, really, when you think about it.

"Is it almost ready?" Josie asks.

She bounces over to me and rests her chin on my shoulder. Well, almost at my shoulder. She's on her tippy-toes and trying to sneak a peek at how the food is coming along.

"Yup." I switch off the stove and move the pan off of the heat. "Just need the serving dish. Can you get it for me, please?"

I nod over to the cabinet out of habit, and she follows the direction while I keep stirring. Once all the food is on the table a minute or so later, we both dig in as if it were the last meal of our lives. We really love our tacos.

"So, are you nervous about starting eighth grade tomorrow?" I ask in between bites.

She shrugs. "No, not really. Should be interesting though, to see if I was able to get the two electives I signed up for."

"Which ones were those? Did you tell me about them?"

"Geez, Mom," she says with a giggle. "Getting old, huh?"

"Ha-ha. Very funny." I stick my tongue out at her. "Watch it, kid. Because the day will come when you'll barely remember what you had for breakfast."

"Mom, I don't eat breakfast."

I cock my head to the side. "You don't?"

She levels me with a stare that says that I damn well know she's not a big breakfast eater. I just love to bust her chops, which must be a rite of passage for a parent. Plus, it's kind of funny to make her think I'm losing my memory every so often.

"Mom, you're not *that* old . . . yet."

I cup my ear and lean in toward her. "What's that you say? Speak up. I can't hear you."

Josie starts to laugh, which gets me laughing, and then I'm all of a sudden choking on my food. She leans over and starts patting me on the back really hard with a look of concern on her face.

I take a quick sip of water before saying, "I'm fine. Just went down the wrong pipe."

"That's what she said."

"Josie, first of all, you don't even know what that means. Secondly, don't go around saying that."

"Aunt Julia says it all the time."

That woman and her mouth. I swear I'm going to kill her. I love her to pieces and she's the best sister-in-law I could have ever hoped to get from my baby brother, Alex, but some of the things that come flying out of her mouth in the presence of children are beyond comprehension.

"I'm not a little girl anymore, Mom. I wish you would stop treating me like one. In case you forgot, you know, because your memory is going already, I'm going to be thirteen in a couple of months."

"Have you gotten your menses yet?" I ask.

"Oh my God! You did not just ask me that in the middle of Taco Tuesday!" she yells while her face turns a shade of red. "And who goes around calling it 'menses' anyway?"

"If you haven't gotten your menses yet, which I know you haven't, then guess what? You're still a little girl and I can tell you what to do. As a matter of fact, I'll be telling you what to do for the rest of your life, so just get used to it. It's my job as your mother."

"Please don't ever say 'menses' again."

"Menses, menses, menses."

Josie's tough act starts to crack, but she tries to keep her laughter from bubbling over too much by going for seconds and ignoring my teasing.

After a moment of Josie building up another taco, I ask, "So you have everything ready for tomorrow? Nothing you can think of that you'll be asking for at the last minute, right?"

"I think so," she says with her mouth full of food. "I mean, I'm pretty sure I'm all set. Although you know how the first day usually goes. Some teacher might have very specific things that weren't on the supply list that I'll end up needing and don't have yet."

"That's fine. I'll take you to the store tomorrow after school if that's the case." I reach across the table for the shredded cheese and then ask, "What are you going to wear?"

"I haven't decided yet," she says. "It's between that powder blue top and the cornflower blue top. I'll decide in the morning."

This has been a point of contention between us. I mean, how difficult is it to find one outfit? The answer to that is that it's nearly impossible. I've been to the mall too many times over the last couple of weeks for it to be anywhere near normal. I've even gone on website after website for her, looking for that just-right outfit that will make some sort of statement on the first day of school. I get it. I really do. I've been there myself when I was her age. But for God's sake, there is absolutely no difference between one blue top versus another top in a slightly lighter shade of blue. Just pick one and stick with it.

"So long as you decide in enough time that I'm not waiting around for you, Your Royal Highness."

Josie wipes her mouth with a napkin, then says, "Of course. I can't be late on the first day of school, Mom."

"You can go ahead and get moving on your shower if you like instead of helping me with the dishes."

"Really? Are you sure, Mom?"

"Yup. But I'm only letting you off the hook with the dishes because I know you have a big day tomorrow . . . and you really need to wash that stuff out of your hair."

Before long, I'm drying off my hands and ready to call it a night. As I walk upstairs to my bedroom, I hear the shower turning on in the hallway bathroom. In my head, I'm already projecting the time for Josie's shower to be in the ballpark of twenty minutes. Which means at the ten-minute mark, I'll have to give the obligatory knock on the door to let her know she's taking too long.

It's like a dance routine every night. And every night I find myself more tired and yearning for my bed earlier and earlier.

Sometimes, when I get too wound up in my own head, I'll get out of bed and pad over to Josie's room, quietly open her bedroom door, and peek in at her for a few seconds while she's sleeping. Just long enough so that all the madness and stress disappears at the sight of her sleeping peacefully in her bed.

I smile to myself as the image flashes in my mind while I fall back onto my bed. The goose-down comforter conforms to my body, and the smell of the lavender scented candle on my nightstand instantly relaxes me. I stretch my arms over my head and glance at my wristwatch. Yup, ten minutes and Josie's still in the shower. Trying to muster up the energy to will myself out of bed and give her the usual warning to wrap things up in there, I hear the shower turn off.

Thank God for tiny miracles.

I get more settled in my bed and turn on the television. I have this thing, it's a sickness really, where I must have the television on all night long. It's practically on mute by the time I fall asleep, but it has to be on. After I had Josie, the random programming in the middle of the night became my company while I changed, fed, cooed, and rocked her back to sleep. Now it's a habit. And there's nobody in here with me to complain about it anyway, so . . .

While channel surfing, I hear a soft knock on my bedroom door. It's Josie. Her hair is still wet, but thankfully all back to its normal color. I would have felt sorry for her if she had to go to school tomorrow with that awful fuchsia in her hair.

"Mom," she says hesitantly.

"Yeah, sweetie, what's wrong?"

She looks worried. And now I'm worried that I've overlooked something that I shouldn't have.

"Nothing's wrong. It's just . . ."

She stops and shyly scans the room before bringing her gaze back to me. My heart starts to race in anxious parent mode.

"Josie, are you sure everything is okay?"

"Yeah. I was just wondering if you wouldn't mind if I slept with you tonight. I mean, it's a big day tomorrow and I might be just a tiny bit nervous about it. And—"

I throw back the comforter and pat the bed with a big smile on my face. "Get in here."

Once she's safely underneath the blanket, I switch off the light and then reach over to kiss her on the forehead.

"Thanks, Mom."

"You're welcome, kid. Now get some sleep. Big day tomorrow and all."

She rolls over, and she's so small that I barely see the movement underneath all the fluff of the comforter covering her body. But then she stops moving and calls out to me, "Hey, Mom?"

"Yes?"

"I love you."

It melts my heart every time. Doesn't matter if I'm having the worst day or the best day, when she says those three little words, it brings a smile to my face and a peace to my mind that is indescribable. "I love you more, sweetie. Good night."

With that, she's asleep with a soft snore in less than ten minutes, and it doesn't take me too long to join her. Tomorrow we'll start this craziness all over again . . . just another day in the life where it's us against the world.

CHAPTER TWO

If I get out of here tonight without falling asleep, it will be a miracle. It's Josie's Back to School Night, which I attend every year during the first week of school, at which I sit in each of her classes to meet her teachers as they give the rundown of the year's classroom objectives.

It sounds awful to say, but some subjects are *sooooo* boring. Like this next one. It's science, according to her schedule, and the teacher will probably drone on and on, and if last year is any indication, he'll look like Bill Nye the Science Guy. Usually, two minutes into the presentation, I'm fighting to stay awake.

Walking with my head down, I trek through the throng of parents until I'm sitting toward the back of the classroom in a seat that was not made to fit an adult's body. Absentmindedly, I start to thumb through the packet of papers, left on each of the desks by Bill Nye, when I hear the door shut and a man's voice say, "Good evening, parents. Welcome to my science class. My name is Mr. Thomas."

My head perks up because that voice . . . it's like nothing I've ever heard before. It's smooth and decadent, like a shot of perfectly aged whiskey that when it hits the back of your throat, the warmth that spreads to your body and makes you want to curl up into a blanket after stretching your limbs like a cat taking an afternoon nap.

And the visual of Bill Nye, sorry, Mr. Thomas, matches the voice, which never seems to be the case where men are concerned. At least I've never seen it happen anywhere as perfectly as this man right in front of me.

He's tall, very tall, and broad shouldered but not bulky or anything, more like athletic. He looks as if he spends a lot of time carrying things, which has paid off in spades from the way his muscular arms flex underneath his clothes. His jet-black hair is combed back perfectly, and there's not one stray hair that I can see from where I'm sitting . . . and I'm really looking. His wire-rimmed eyeglasses only prove to showcase his equally dark dead-of-night brown eyes. Oh my, *Sherlock* was right: brainy *is* the new sexy.

But the pièce de résistance is the clothes. My God, the clothes. My most naughty teenage fantasy made real: he's wearing a tweed suit like an old-school college professor. Like Professor Indiana Jones himself came to life and stepped off the movie screen and is now standing right in front of me in all his adorably dorky, aloof hotness, packaged perfectly in the guise of a random science teacher in Anytown, USA.

Mr. Thomas is drop-dead gorgeous. And I'm so going to get an *A* in this class.

Wait! What the hell am I thinking?

I'm not getting an *A* in anything. I'm just going to chalk up this little drool fest to the fact that I'm not usually attracted to men I meet. I do have very singular tastes and apparently this man fits into my tastes quite well. Perfectly, actually. Like a glove.

Jeez! There I go again.

Okay, Vanessa, I think to myself as calmly as possible, *stop thinking about Mr. Thomas like he's grade-A meat and listen to what he has to say.*

"I've left the class syllabus on the desks for you to take home and review, and if you have any questions, please don't hesitate to send me an e-mail," he says with quiet authority. "Also, today your children should have brought home a consent form for you to sign and turn in by the end of next week before we begin working on our first lab assignment."

Consent form? Josie didn't mention anything like that when I dropped her off at my brother's house so her aunt Julia could babysit while I was here tonight.

A hand shoots up on the far side of the classroom. Mr. Thomas nods subtly in the person's direction. God, he's smooth.

"What is the consent form for?" the parent asks.

"It's simply to allow your child to use a Bunsen burner during my class. If you choose to say no, that's fine too. We can work around it if need be."

Mr. Thomas shoves his hands in his pants pockets, which doesn't help me in the slightest while I try to keep my composure. Because it only accentuates his athletic frame and showcases how well he wears his suit even more.

I scan the room to see if I'm the only person entranced by this man, and lo and behold, I'm not. There is another woman leaning forward in her child-sized seat, who looks as if she is in rapt attention. If there was a nuclear bomb going off outside, nothing would disturb her from the more than obvious leering she's giving this guy. She's wearing head to toe coordinated shades of brown, even going so far as to top it all off with a fake flower pinned in her hair in a dark chocolate color.

Then I realize I must look like that to anyone who happens to spare me a fleeting glance. So I quickly turn my head back to Mr. Thomas just when he's looking right at me.

The corners of his mouth tilt up in a friendly smile that sends a tingle up my spine and makes me smile right back at him, which is so unlike me, but I can't seem to help myself. In fact, I'm so enraptured by him that it's as if there is no one else in the room. For one fleeting moment, the world seems to fall away, and it's just the two of us in this classroom with only the sea of desks between us. He's about to say something to me, and I'm waiting with bated breath until a woman's shrill voice breaks the spell.

"Oh, Mr. Thomas," the woman says. I turn my head even though I already know it's the other woman in the class who is entranced by him. "I was wondering if you were looking for any parents to volunteer to be class parent? I would be so happy to lend a helping hand."

A couple of parents sitting near me chuckle and joke to each other in hushed voices about how they bet she wants to lend a helping hand. It's at this point that I start to gather my things and decide to be the very first person out of this classroom as soon as he dismisses us. Because the last thing I would want is to be the butt of any joke if they saw me looking at him like I've been. Or if they even catch a glimpse of my face, which must reflect what I'm sure is a tell-all look of complete adoration.

"I don't think that will be necessary," he responds to the woman diplomatically. "But thank you for volunteering."

Mr. Thomas then turns his attention to all the parents and says, "Thank you so much for coming out tonight, and I very much look forward to teaching your children this year. Good night."

Like I have ants in my pants, I make my way to the door and out of the classroom as fast as I can, trying not to sneak one last glance at Mr. Thomas and failing miserably. But he's surrounded by a sea of people, so I don't have to acknowledge him. What would I say anyway? I'm horrible at that kind of stuff, and my game is not the kind that people equate to swagger. It's more . . . Monopoly. Lest I forget, he's my daughter's teacher. So there is no scenario in the world where it would be okay for me to even toy with the idea of a relationship with him. It's unethical and just plain wrong.

Plus, Josie would kill me! Oh my God, would she ever.

I laugh to myself as I make my way out of the school and into the parking lot, which is already overflowing with parents rushing to get home to their families or trying to get home in time to watch *American Idol*, which starts in about fifteen minutes, according to a few parents I overheard. I roll my eyes, since I gave up on that show years ago when they were obviously choosing the wrong people to go to the next round. I would be so incensed while watching it that I could barely function, much less sleep after an episode. So to ease my escalating blood pressure and to ensure that my neighbors wouldn't call the police due to high-pitched screaming and yelling and carrying on, I did everyone a favor by quitting while I was ahead. My blood pressure thanks me every day.

I pull up to my brother's house a short while later, and when I approach the front door, I can hear my beautifully adorable, deliciously sweet, and cherubic two-and-a-half-year-old niece, Violet, giggling clear as a bell, followed by Julia's loud, booming voice shouting, "Violet! You need to put your pajamas on *over* your pull-up, not the other way around! Alex, help! I'm tagging out! It's your turn!" These days, I revel a little in seeing Alex and Julia go through the same exact struggles I did years ago with Josie. Only Violet doesn't belong to me, so I can laugh about it. Heartily, I might add.

My brother, Alex, shouts back, "You can't just tag out! This isn't WrestleMania!"

I'm practically doubled over laughing as I slip the key they gave me—in case of emergencies only, but these types of situations qualify—into the lock and slowly open the door. Immediately I spot Violet sitting crisscross-applesauce on the foyer floor. She's attempting to comb her freshly washed long, naturally curly, Beach Blonde hair with not much success, as both her parents are now calling out her name. She's wearing Princess Elsa pajamas, but her pull-up is over them instead of the other way around.

"Hey there, Violet." I crouch down to her level. "Whatcha doing?"

"Auntie Nessa," she says with a big smile that makes my heart melt before she hands me the comb with a defeated look on her face. "I was trying to be a big girl. Can you help?"

"Of course, sweetie." I take the comb from her and open my arms so she can climb on, and I walk her over to the couch. When I sit down, I stand her up in front of me. Her big blue eyes, which are as a bright as a cloudless sky, look back at me in amusement as I take in her outfit. "Now, Miss Violet, I know you know you're wearing that thing wrong. So why don't we fix it first?"

She nods her head in agreement and starts to giggle. "Close your eyes, Auntie Nessa."

I shut my eyes for what feels like a whole five minutes as I hear my niece struggle to put her pajamas and pull-up on correctly. "Ta-da," she says loudly. "You can open them."

"Very good, Violet." She still has her pants off and her shirt is hiked up now, halfway up her belly. "Can I help now?"

Violet turns around so that I can begin combing her hair. I hear the sound of footsteps approaching from down the hallway.

"There you are," Julia says. "Didn't you hear your father and me calling for you?"

"I want Auntie Nessa to help," Violet says. Julia smiles and I swear it's uncanny how much it's just like her daughter's.

"Do you mind?" she asks me while I'm still combing Violet's hair.

"Not at all. I miss these days."

Julia takes a seat on the other end of the sofa in exhaustion after picking up her daughter's pajama pants off of the floor. "She is giving us a run for our money. Do they ever stop? I mean, I love her to pieces and everything, but please, tell me the truth . . . does it get any easier?"

"Nope."

"Gee, thanks, Vanessa," she says. "You couldn't even lie a little bit to your own sister-in-law?"

"Enjoy it while it lasts, Julia. Pretty soon she'll be going out with her friends and then off to college and then getting married and—"

"Whoa, whoa, whoa," she says with her hands up. "Slow down there, Debbie Downer. Nobody's talking about college and marriage. I meant just this phase where it seems like up is down and it's the funniest thing in the world to her to drive her parents crazy."

Smiling, I glance over to Julia, who looks like she's been in a battle with a water hose. Undoubtedly, this was due to Violet splashing in the bathtub. "Maybe a little easier."

"Can we trade?" she asks me with a devious grin. "I'll take Josie and you take Violet."

Violet snaps out of whatever spell she was under and jumps onto her mother's lap. "No! I want to stay with you and Daddy forever!"

"Trust me, baby," she says to her daughter. "Daddy isn't going to let you out of his sight. Like, ever. You got nothing to worry about."

"Promise?" Violet asks, worrying her lip.

"Promise, baby," Julia says solemnly and places a kiss on her daughter's forehead. "Now, do your mommy a big favor and put your pants on so you can get ready for bed."

Violet practically bounces off her mother and comes back toward me with her pants in hand. "Auntie Nessa, can you help?"

"Of course, but first . . ."

I lunge for Violet and catch her unprepared with an assault of raspberries on her exposed stomach. She laughs and laughs and struggles to get me to stop, and when I do it's only because she's at the point where her laughter is almost silent and her face turns a slight shade of rosy red.

Pulling away but keeping her in my arms, I say, "You're turning violet, Violet!"

"Yeah, like that's not getting old after the first million times you've said it to her," Alex says, appearing in the living room at the tail end of my tickling attack.

"Daddy!" Violet yells and raises her arms for him. "Help me, Daddy!"

Alex scoops her up easily in his arms and hugs her to him as if she were the most precious thing in the world. And when I look over at Julia, who is watching this whole exchange, her face is practically glowing in adoration of her husband's love of their daughter. For a second I feel a hint of jealousy, because Josie has never experienced this. Granted, Alex has been her father figure since the day she was born and is the closest thing to a dad she will ever know in her life. To Alex's credit, he has gone above and beyond anything I could have ever wanted for Josie. But at the end of the day, it's not the same thing. And that makes me sad for her . . . for us.

"Will you put her to bed?" Julia asks Alex.

He nods, then bends down so Julia can give Violet a kiss good night. He does the same for me before setting off down the hall with her tangled up in his arms like a little monkey hugging a tree. Julia and I watch them walk away and hear Violet ask him, "Daddy, tell me the story about Max and the wild stuff?"

We don't get to hear Alex's answer, but if I had to guess, if she had asked him to jump off a bridge, he would ask which one and how high; that's how smitten he is with her and how much Violet has him wrapped around her finger.

"I think my ovaries just exploded," Julia says.

"Ew, gross," I say. "That's my brother still."

"Fair enough."

"Where is Josie?" I ask.

Julia leans back and props her feet up on the coffee table, looking as if she could fall asleep at any moment. "Last time I checked, before I tried to do a battle royal in the bathtub with Violet, Josie had her earbuds in and was watching something on TV in the other room. If you give me just one full minute to sit here with my feet up, I swear I'll go get her for you."

Laughing, I indulge my sister-in-law in the brief moment of silence that to her must seem like a luxury nowadays. I mean, I could very well just get Josie and be on my merry way, but I kind of like just sitting here, closing my eyes, and letting my mind go blank and not thinking about one single solitary thing.

But the funniest thing happens. Instead of going blank, a thought pops into my mind. Actually, it's not a thought, it's a person . . . one very specific, handsome person: Mr. Thomas, science teacher.

The next thing to come out of my mouth is even more unexpected. "Julia?"

"Hmm?" she answers.

"Do you think Indiana Jones is hot?"

Without missing a beat, Julia answers with a question. "Are we talking before or after Ally McBeal cut off his balls and slapped an earring on his ass?"

My eyes fly open and I look at her. She's still in complete and utter repose and doesn't seem at all caught off guard by my question.

"What are you talking about?" I ask.

"You're asking me if Harrison Ford is hot, yes?" I mumble a yes, and then she opens her eyes and calmly says, "Well, if we're talking about before Ally got her hands on him, yes, he was so utterly hot it was almost disgusting. But if we're talking about after she got her grubby little paws on him and ruined it for the rest of all woman-kind, then no, he's as far away from hot as you could possibly get."

I rack my brain for a second before saying, "Before. Yes, definitely before the whole Ally thing happened to him."

"Well, then, you know my answer. Hot, superhot." She closes her eyes again before quickly opening one of them to look at me. "Why are you asking me this anyway?"

"No reason."

Ugh, I answered way too fast. And by the severely wicked smile that is now growing on Julia's face, I know she knows that I know something that she doesn't and won't let up until she does.

"You dirty little liar," she says and pulls her legs off of the coffee table. "Tell me everything."

"There's nothing to tell." I pretend to look at the watch that doesn't exist on my wrist. "Oh, would you look at that, time to get Josie and go home."

I stand up and call out to Josie, then remember that she has her earbuds in, so I walk toward the television room. But that's enough time for Julia to start following me and peppering me with a series of questions. "Who is this Indiana Jones look-alike? Where did you meet him? Are you going out on a date with him?"

Ignoring her is not an option, so I stop abruptly, which makes Julia run right into my back. As casually as I can muster, I say, "It's nothing and no, I am not going out with anyone. So there really isn't anything to tell, I promise."

By the look of confusion on her face, I can tell my explanation wasn't enough, so I add, "But as soon as there is something to tell, I swear you'll be the first person I call."

Her face beams with a ridiculous goofy smile, but I don't have the heart to tell her that there will never be a thing to share. If just the promise of nothing is enough to put her off, then so be it.

Josie sees us coming her way and pops out her earbuds. "Hey, Mom, how was it?"

"Good, sweetie," I say. "We've got to get going home though. Can you start packing up your things?"

Josie answers by getting all of her stuff ready, and in another minute we're saying our good-byes to Julia, with both of us telling her to pass on our good-byes to Alex and Violet.

But before we make our escape, Julia grabs my elbow with superhuman strength as Josie is making her way to my car.

"I don't know what's going on with you, but something is going on," she whispers, yet manages to make it sound like a threat.

"Julia—"

She lets go of my arm and puts her hands up to stop me. "I'm not saying I need to know everything. What I'm trying to say is—and obviously doing the worst job possible—is that if you need me for anything, I'm here for you."

And in that instant, and as crazy as it seems, I feel a closeness to my sister-in-law that I've never experienced before. I know it doesn't make sense, because it's just this one little thing about a guy who she has no clue about and probably never will, but it's true. I don't have a sister and neither does Julia. And through marriage, she has become the sister I had always wished for and probably vice versa for her. I can only imagine that this is what sisters are supposed to be like: sharing and caring for each other, yet remaining close friends through thick and thin and being there for the other whenever the time calls for it.

"You'll be the first person I call if Indiana Jones shows up on my doorstep."

She claps her hands together and says one last good night to me before closing the door. After we arrive home safe and sound, Josie goes to bed in her room and me in mine, and I'm still smiling at the exchange between Julia and me, because if anything, I think being friends, like real friends with someone, is the beginning of opening myself up for other things in my life.

CHAPTER THREE

Ever since I was a little girl, I've dreamed that one day I'd be sitting on the banks of the Seine in Paris with my sketchbook in hand, living as an artist. From as far back as I can remember, I've had an ability to flesh out my thoughts on paper, either in charcoal or watercolors. It's just always come easily to me. I used to sit for hours, drawing the flowers outside my mother's kitchen windowsill. Taking great care to get the colors and shading right and the way the petals bent just so whenever the wind would pick up. Sometimes something as random as pieces of broken glass on the concrete would get my attention, and I'd take a mental snapshot and then start drawing it in variations when I got home, until my wrists were sore and my hands were nearly black with charcoal. My mom likes to take credit for this. And she probably should. She always nurtured my love of painting and drawing, fostering it with art classes, taking my brother and me to exhibits from a very early age, and encouraging me to push myself past my limits to see the fruits of my labor.

Needless to say, I never envisioned myself working part-time at a construction company as an office manager. Then again, I never pictured myself being a single mom either. But that's the way the cookie crumbled for me.

My father owns said construction company: Holt Construction. So yes, I took the nepotism route. I'm not ashamed by it either.

When he offered me the job, at first I was hesitant since I hadn't ever worked in an office environment. I'd been waitressing here and there to supplement my income as an artist and making ends meet just fine. But living on tips, not to mention the hours, was nowhere near a suitable option for me once Josie came into the picture. And as much as I pride myself on being independent—getting an art scholarship for college, working at the local pub near campus to pay for my books and art supplies, never asking my parents for a dime and instead selling some of my pieces at street fairs to put food on the table—I couldn't smack a gift horse in the mouth when my father approached me with this job. I think it takes a lot of courage to be able to admit to oneself that you can't do all of it alone. That saying "it takes a village to raise a child" is remarkably true.

During the school year my days usually begin around five in the morning. After I hit the snooze bar a couple of times, I drag myself out of bed and onto the treadmill for my daily two-mile run, then take a quick shower before I wake Josie up by six thirty. After I've warned her that I'm waiting to leave at least four times, she's usually done getting ready for school. I'll drop her off and head to the office, which is about thirty minutes away.

As the office manager, I'm supposed to be in the office before the rest of the staff. What ends up actually happening is that the barista at Starbucks—who has been making my salted caramel mochas for the last five years—starts chatting with me, and before I know it, I'm getting to the office at exactly the same time as everyone else. I don't take a lunch hour or a break, really, and maybe sneak one empanada at my desk from the roach coach that makes the rounds of the corporate park. On most days, I work straight through until it's time to pick up Josie after school or after whatever club meeting she has on any given day of the week. If we don't have to stop anywhere, like my brother's house, or my parents' house, or the grocery store, we're usually home by four o'clock in the afternoon. She'll do her homework while I make dinner. We eat together, and then it's back to bed and I'm hitting the rewind button to do it all over again the next day. Basically, my life is like Bill Murray's in *Groundhog Day*.

On the weekend, all bets are off. For one, we sleep in. I've trained Josie well in that she likes to stay in bed as long as humanly possible, just like me. But the best part of the weekend is that it allows me the luxury of time to paint or draw, sometimes all day if I'm lucky.

If I didn't have this outlet, I'd probably lose my mind. I decompress, but more than that, it's a way to express myself on canvas. As an artist, albeit a part-time one at this point in my life, it's a gift to be able to pour my heart and soul into a piece and see it come to life right before my very eyes. Even if it's only for my eyes. Whether or not the pieces I create are shared with the world or stay with me forever is not the point. It's the road I take to get to the final product that makes life that much more satisfying.

With the anticipation of possibly working in my studio this weekend putting a smile on my face, I start to wind down my day at the office before I have to leave to pick up Josie. It's a Friday, which is movie night at our house. I usually pick up some takeout, and then we plop ourselves in front of the living room television to watch and eat dinner in our pajamas. We alternate who gets to pick what we watch, and this time it's my turn. Even though I dread how fast my little girl is not so little anymore, there are some advantages to her growing up, one of which is not to have to sit through awful kid movies—Disney and Pixar films excluded, of course. I'm a sucker for the Beast and that old curmudgeon in *Up*.

As I'm mentally cataloging the favorites in my Netflix account to choose from later tonight, my dad calls out to me from his office. "Vanessa, can you stop in here for a minute before you leave for the day, please?"

Out of habit, I stuff a pencil into the makeshift bun in my hair and swivel the chair away from my desk. "I'll be right there, Dad."

I cringe after realizing I called him "Dad" in front of the rest of the office staff. I try to keep our relationship in the office professional by calling him Mr. Holt, but sometimes I slip up.

"Sorry, I mean, Mr. Holt," I say as I walk into his office and take a seat.

"You don't have to call me that, Vanessa. It sounds ridiculous, and everybody thinks so, and so do you." He pauses and lifts his head from the monitor to give me a wry smile.

"I know, but it doesn't feel right to remind everyone every single day that I only got this job because I'm your daughter."

"Vanessa, if you weren't any good at this job, I would have fired you years ago whether you're my daughter or not."

I chuckle. "No you wouldn't."

My dad doesn't laugh at all. "I fired your brother, didn't I?"

"No you didn't. He quit when he bought the gallery, and then you 'fired' him to save face in front of them." I jerk a thumb over my shoulder to the rest of the office staff.

Alex had worked for my dad's construction company every single summer from the time he was twelve years old until a few years after he graduated from college. It was then that he had saved up enough money to buy his own art gallery in South Beach. When he finally told my dad that he was quitting, my dad was so upset that his only son wouldn't be taking over the family business that he "fired" him. They didn't speak for a week, until my mom stepped in to clear the air between them. Ever since then, my dad likes to remind me that he technically fired Alex, but we both know it's nowhere near the truth.

"Semantics." He clears his throat and then says, "I just wanted to check in before you left to make sure you didn't need anything from me, because I'll be away on vacation until Wednesday."

"Did you sign all those purchase order forms I left for you earlier?"

"I just finished." He hands me a pile of papers across his desk. "Anything else?"

"I don't think so. If you can just check in with the foreman on the Chamberlin job before you hit the road today, I'd appreciate it. It will save me the headache of having to field calls from both sides come Monday morning."

My dad smiles. "You got it. But you do realize they will still call no matter what I tell them, right?"

"I know." I get up and go to leave his office. Stopping at the door, I turn and lean on the door frame. "Where are you going anyway?"

"I'm taking your mother away to a little B and B in the Keys for a little R and R, if you know what I mean." He winks and then laughs.

"That's disgusting, Dad. TMI."

"TMI?" he asks. "Is that some lingo the kids are saying these days?"

"Yes, it means too much information."

My dad stands up and walks around his desk toward me. "Vanessa, when are you going to be going to a little B and B in the Keys for a little R and R?"

"Dad!"

"Shhh! Keep your voice down." He grabs my arm and pulls me forward so he can shut the door and give us some privacy. "Vanessa, your mother and I are worried about you. All you do is this and Josie. All day, every day. You need to get out more, meet people, and be social."

"That's not true," I say on a shaky breath. "I do lots of things."

My father gives me a look that makes me feel like a little girl all over again. "Sweetheart, you know your mother and I want nothing but the best for you, right?"

"Yes."

"I—I mean *we*—wonder when you're ever going to get back on that saddle."

I cross my arms to keep my heart from exploding out of my chest. My cheeks blaze red in embarrassment. Because the very last thing any thirtysomething woman wants is her father wondering when she's ever going to be getting some in this lifetime.

"Dad, I'm happy. Why is that so hard for you and Mom, or anyone for that matter, to believe?"

And I am. I'm supercalifragilisticexpialidocious every day. Well, technically not every day . . . but close enough so I don't feel there is anything that is missing from my life.

My dad is still staring at me with concern in his eyes, as if the more times I say it out loud, the more I'm trying to convince myself that it's true.

"I swear, Dad, I'm very happy. Everything is just fine as it is. Plus, what kind of message would I be sending to your granddaughter if I started bringing men in and out of her life?"

He rubs his chin thoughtfully and opens his mouth to answer. "Um . . ."

"Exactly. So please let me live my life, since I've been doing just fine all this time. And who says I need a man in my life to complete it anyway?"

"Well—"

"Well what, Dad?"

"Well, I never said you needed a man to complete your life, Vanessa. I simply was trying to get you to loosen up a bit. Go out with your friends. Do something instead of this." He waves his hand in the air dramatically around us. At least he has the sense to look a little sheepish.

"Dad, I appreciate your concern, I really do . . . and Mom's, but I swear, I'm fine. Please stop worrying about me." I lean forward and kiss him on the cheek. "Go ahead and pick up Mom for your little getaway. I'll hold down the fort like I always do while you're gone and see you in a few days."

Before he can say anything, I open the door to his office and walk back to my desk with purpose in every stride. I can feel his eyes burning a hole in the back of my head while I start gathering my belongings to leave for the day.

I make sure to say good night and the usual "have a good weekend" to everyone I pass until I'm out the door and under the blazing late afternoon Miami sun. It's then I take a big gulp of hot air through my nose and blow it out from my mouth. I do this one more time to relax enough to operate the heavy machinery necessary to pick up my daughter from school. Nobody should be behind the wheel when they're this upset. I mean, it's a recipe for disaster. I can't even think straight, that's how upset I am right now.

The hard truth of it is that I don't have many friends. I had Josie when I was twenty-four years old. My friends at the time were busy living it up, dating, and having a ball. And there I was, trying to find the right formula for my newborn so that she wouldn't throw up on me every three hours after she finished a bottle. So slowly but surely, the friends I did have fell by the wayside. Josie came first. I barely have time as it is to think about how I don't have friends. But I have my family. They've always been supportive of Josie and me, and have been there through everything.

And as far as dating or a relationship goes, no on both counts. As a single parent, to a girl especially, I can't be flip about who I bring into our lives, our home. I've come to terms with this. It's taken me years, but it gets easier to be alone. In fact, I rather enjoy it. It's kind of hard to break out of the habit after almost thirteen years of it. Who knows? Maybe I'll start dating when Josie finally has to put me in a home so I don't cramp her style.

Walking toward my parked car, I start to relax. This isn't the first time that one of my parents has tried to have a "come to Jesus" talk with me about my nonsocial life. My parents should take their cue from Alex, who knows better than to even say one word about it anymore. But sadly, every time they see an opportunity, they strike, and they strike hard. It's even worse when they gang up on me. I've feigned illnesses at family parties a few times to get away from their incessant nagging.

I understand my parents' concern. But honestly, when are they going to get sick of having the same conversation, over and over again, when obviously nobody is listening? Or, more importantly, why don't they realize that I've been doing just fine for years, and that I'm completely okay with my life?

And I am. I'm okay . . . with everything. As is.

I've been so absorbed with this latest conversation about my not having a life that before I know it, I'm pulling up to Josie's school. Luckily, I don't have to text her to let her know I'm here since she's already outside waiting for me. She's sitting underneath a palm tree with a couple of her friends, looking as happy as I've ever seen her.

Josie gathers up her things and starts walking toward the car. But halfway here, she stops and says something to her friends, who giggle and cross their fingers. She turns around again and walks the rest of the distance, then opens the passenger-side door, letting the stifling hot air suffocate the car for the two seconds or so she has the door open before slamming it shut and we're on the road again.

"How was your day?" I ask.

"Good, thanks," she says cheerfully. "How was yours?"

"Good. The usual." I put my turn signal on to make a left onto Sunset Avenue but get stuck at the light. I turn my head to look at her. She's on her cell phone, texting, when I ask, "So, do you have any preference on what kind of movie I pick tonight? I'm thinking something scary or maybe something really sappy. What do you think?"

"Mom, I—"

"Oh, I know," I say as the light turns green and I'm finally able to make my left turn. "How about a classic, like *What's Up Doc?*"

"Well, I was thinking—"

"Or we can do *Grease*? You like that one a lot. I have to admit, I still do too. I honestly cannot wait until you're old enough to watch

Saturday Night Fever, so you can see for yourself the way I like to remember John Travolta. I watched reruns of *Welcome Back, Kotter* as a kid, but he was—"

"Mom," Josie says a little more abruptly than usual. "I actually was going to ask you if you would let me spend the night at Carrie's house tonight."

"Tonight? But it's our movie night." I can't help the disappointment that leaks into my voice.

"I know it's our movie night," she says quietly. "But Carrie is having Lorelei over to spend the night and we were hoping . . . I was hoping . . . that you'd say yes because I'd really like to go."

"But it's our thing," I say more to myself than to her and regret saying it out loud as soon as the words are out of my mouth. "I'm sorry, kid. I didn't mean it like that. What I meant to say is that we usually have our movie night on Fridays, and I was really looking forward to unwinding with you tonight."

"Mom, you kind of said the same thing two ways."

"I'm sorry, you're right, I did."

"And you know, it's not really fair to make me sit around and do nothing just because you don't have anything to do either."

"Just because you're not getting your way, Josie, doesn't mean you can speak to me however you like. I'm still your mother."

"Sorry," she mumbles.

Suddenly I feel incredibly guilty for wanting to keep her all to myself. I can't help but think that I've been banking on this very idea, that Josie would want to always hang out with me. But let's be honest, what almost-teenager wants to do that? I know at her age I was always at a friend's house and vice versa. And Josie has friends, lots of them, who she sees quite often outside of school. So who am I to keep her from having a social life simply because I don't have—

No. Not even going to think it.

We're quiet for the rest of the drive until we're about a block away from my town house. As I'm pulling onto our street, I sneak a quick glance over to Josie, who's sitting like a slouched sack of potatoes in the passenger seat while staring mindlessly out the window.

"Josie," I say softly while pulling into the driveway. I see the expectant look on her face, because she knows what I'm about to say. Because I know that this is going to be the first of many times that I have to start letting her go and live her life. Because this is a very big step, and it's only going to get increasingly difficult for me to get a handle on it. But I'm going to try. "Sweetheart, go ahead and text Carrie and have her mom call me to work out the details about the sleepover tonight and—"

She lunges across the center console and hugs me so tightly while saying over and over, "Thank you, thank you, thank you! You're the best mom ever!"

Later that night, after Josie has been picked up by Carrie's mom and I'm sitting on the couch alone with the television on, a glass of white wine in one hand and remote in the other, staring at the screen and not absorbing one iota of what's being shown, I come to the sad realization that my parents are completely right. I don't have any semblance of a social life. Why it has taken me so long to realize this, I have no idea. Why I didn't want to accept it before today, who knows. Probably because I've been content just going on about my business and making sure Josie goes about hers. But I'm not going to have a pity party. There is no point in feeling sorry for myself or having a smidgeon of jealousy of my daughter's social life.

Maybe it doesn't have to be all or nothing. Maybe I can start living my life a little bit at a time while Josie lives hers. We can still have our time together, but I can do other things while she does hers. And maybe, just maybe, we can have the best of both worlds.

CHAPTER FOUR

Here's the thing about a plan: you actually have to form a plan before you can take any action on it.

Which is why two weeks after my epiphany on the couch, I still haven't done anything to set the wheels in motion toward bettering my social state. Between my dad's absence from the office and Josie and me getting into the swing of the new school year, I just haven't had the time. So another week from now I think I'll see the light at the edge of the horizon.

Just have to plan some time for myself to formulate the plan.

But, today . . . well, today is a day that I look forward to every year. I've been attending the South Miami Rotary Art Festival since as far back as I can remember, and for the past few years, I've been able to show my pieces and sell some too.

It started out as a dare from my mother. She pushed and pushed me to display my work until I eventually applied to have my own booth. Now, five years later, I look forward to it like a kid on Christmas morning. And to be honest, even if I don't sell one single piece during the course of the two days I work this event, I'll still be over the moon ecstatic to be considered a part of the community of artists who come from all over the area to participate in it.

"Are you almost ready, Mom?" Josie calls out from the front door. "We're burning daylight here."

"Very funny!" I shout back.

I'm studying the last few pieces I completed recently to see if they are worth taking. There is one piece in particular that I'm not sure about yet. But in the end, I decide to grab it and place it in my portfolio just in case I change my mind.

It doesn't take long to get to the event, and with Josie's help, which she does every year, I'm set up in no time and waiting for the so-called doors to open so that the patrons can walk up and down the closed off road and peruse everyone's work.

About ten minutes to start time, Josie asks, "Mom, is it okay if I walk right over there to get something to drink?"

I follow the finger she's pointing to my left and down the block to a Starbucks that's already bustling with customers.

"Yes," I answer and start to dig into my purse. "Can you pick me up a coffee too?"

She smiles and takes the twenty-dollar bill I hand her and then bounces off. I keep my eyes trained on her and her swinging pony-tail until she's well inside the store.

While she's gone, I open my portfolio and look over the sketch I'm uncertain about. Sometimes I name my pieces, depending on my mood at creation or if it's directly inspired by something I saw or read. In this particular case, I had just finished watching, of all things, *Maleficent*. Afterward, it left me thinking about the phrase "true love's kiss." To the point that I became a bit obsessed with it.

True love's kiss . . .

It sounds so innocent and hopeful, and taken at face value it's a chaste promise of romance and never-ending, undying love brought on by a simple kiss between two people. However, when you think about it, at least as much as I have, when exactly would you know with all the certainty in your heart that a kiss is *the* true love's kiss? Does it exist merely in fairy tales? Or, if the right man comes along, does his love for you and all the passion in his heart somehow flow through that barely there brush of lips against yours, until your own heart is overflowing with an emotion that you've never felt before? And as a result of this one little kiss, will you fall head over heels and madly in love with this person, forsaking all others for the rest of your life and vice versa?

The dreamer in me loves the allure of the fantasy. However, the realist in me has a hard time wrapping my head around the whole idea because, really? One kiss could have that much power? I highly doubt it.

But the dreamer side won out and I decided to bring the phrase to life, so to speak, in my own interpretation of it within this sketch. However, every time I look at it, I feel as if there is something missing. The more I look at it, the more puzzled I feel, and I end up putting it away again until I can study it further.

"Here you go, Mom," Josie says, breaking me out of my thoughts and handing me my coffee.

"Thanks, kid."

"Oh, I like that one," she says in admiration. "Where are you going to display it?"

I take a sip of my coffee before answering, "I'm not sure I am."

"Why not? It's beautiful."

"You think so?" I ask. "I'm not sure it's even done."

"Yeah, I love it. Especially the red highlights around the lips for the couple. You usually never use any color other than black for a sketch, so it really stands out to me."

Josie carefully takes the sketch off of my worktable and holds it up to eye level. She gazes at it for a few seconds before looking over the edge of the paper with a beaming smile. "It's romantic."

Laughing a little, I say, "It's supposed to be. I called it *True Love's Kiss*."

"I think you should display it right over . . . there," she says, pointing at a spot at the front section of the booth.

Josie then takes the sketch and, after some minor rearranging, places it alongside another one of my favorites. "There, that's perfect," she announces proudly.

"I'll tell you what," I say to her. "If you're able to sell that one, I'll split the profits with you."

She rubs the palm of her right hand against the denim shorts she's wearing, then offers it up to me to shake, which she does with surprising strength and certainty in her eyes. "You've got yourself a deal," she says.

For the next couple of hours, there's a steady stream of attendees. Some stop in their straw hats with drinks in hand or a makeshift fan to ward off the heat, thoughtfully browsing until moseying down to the next artist's booth. Others stroll by with friends, simply enjoying the gorgeous warm weather that we're blessed with during the fall months. And then there are the true art aficionados that I see year after year who come by to chat about what I've been up to and look over my work, usually buying a piece or two.

I'm in the middle of talking to Elizabeth, a regular attendee who always ends up taking a couple of my pieces, when I look over her shoulder and notice Josie talking to a man and a woman. Their backs are to me, but at first glance, it looks like they're a couple who clearly know each other well, enjoying the day, as evidenced by their obvious closeness when the woman places her hand gently on the man's back and then pats him in a loving manner. Josie's face breaks out into a tooth-bearing grin as she moves past them, and they follow her a few short steps toward the far corner of the booth.

A few long, wavy, dark-blonde strands have escaped my ponytail, so I tuck them behind my ear and try not to seem too distracted by Josie and the couple. I notice that she's purposely directing their attention to *True Love's Kiss*.

She's really trying to make good on that deal.

I try to hide my laughter, but Elizabeth notices and asks, "What's so funny, Vanessa?"

"Oh, it's nothing, really," I tell her. "It's just that Josie is trying to make some money for herself."

Elizabeth spins around to see Josie showing the couple the artwork in question. "She's a natural-born salesperson," she says and hands me the money for her own selections. "Looks like she's made a sale for you. Good for her."

The couple, actually the man, is going through his wallet and taking out a few bills, which he hands to Josie, who smiles like a cat that ate the whole canary. It's then that I see the profile of the man in question, and to my surprise, it's Mr. Thomas, Josie's science teacher. And to my ever-loving dismay and embarrassment, my heart starts to pound in my chest like a bass drum in a marching band.

Josie catches me staring at the exchange and excitedly waves me over. Which just makes my heart palpitate that much more, and for what exactly? Am I feeling this way because he looks the way he does? His khaki shorts and checkered polo shirt with the sleeves rolled up showcase his tanned and toned forearms and athletic legs. Or is it because I'm jealous of the woman he's keeping company with? I don't know him well enough to feel either way, but I can't just ignore him either.

"Excuse me, Elizabeth," I say. "I'll be right back."

"Of course, of course," she answers as I'm already starting to reluctantly walk away.

Mr. Thomas and his girlfriend both turn around to watch me walk toward them, and with every step that brings me closer, my palms begin to sweat more and more before my anxiety hits an all-time high. Because the way he's looking at me isn't quite right, to put it mildly. It's . . . it's like he's appreciating me. And that can't be right, especially with the girlfriend standing next to him.

"Mr. Thomas," I say by way of introduction. "I would have never pegged you for an art lover."

He smiles, but Josie cuts in before he can answer. "Mom, I sold your *True Love's Kiss* piece!"

"Is that what it's called?" Mr. Thomas asks me. "And please, call me Cameron."

"Yes, I thought Josie would have mentioned that to you before you bought it."

The girlfriend speaks up finally. "She never got around to that. Cameron here," she says with a grin and pointing an accusatory finger at him, "didn't need much convincing once your daughter showed it to him."

"My apologies on behalf of my sister," Mr. Thomas says in slight embarrassment.

Oh, she's his sister. Interesting.

"I'm sorry, let me introduce myself. I'm Natalie, Cameron's always teasing older sister."

She puts out her hand and I take it in mine, trying very hard not to let my face betray that I'm pleasantly surprised by this development.

"So, Mr. Thomas—"

"Cameron, please," he says, cutting me off politely.

"Sorry, Cameron." The name rolls off my tongue with a bit of hesitation. "You're an art lover then?"

"I wouldn't say that." He pauses and looks over the sketch thoughtfully. When he turns his eyes to mine again, he quietly says, "But I certainly can appreciate beauty when I see it."

Is he talking about the painting still? I like to think that I'm fairly intelligent, but even I don't know if he means his appreciation of my work or . . . oh my God, is he actually flirting with me?

No, don't even think it, Vanessa, I tell myself before smiling at his praise.

My eyes latch on to Josie's for a brief moment, and hers quickly switch over to look at Cameron, who's watching me closely. Then she switches back to me and then back to him again. All the while, the corners of her lips are curling up in a devious smile. I frown a little in confusion, and with my eyes try to ask her why she's so amused.

Cameron's sister, Natalie, clears her throat dramatically to break the silence and says, "I was just telling Josie how Cameron never buys stuff like this. He's usually buying another Death Star or something for his Geeks-R-Us collection."

"I wouldn't go that far, Natalie," he says under his breath.

"Yeah, right," she says dismissively, then turns back to me and starts talking a mile a minute. "So, we were walking along enjoying the day and bumped into your beautiful daughter, Josie, here, who turns out is a student of my brother's." Natalie takes a quick breath, then keeps on going. "But you already knew that. Anyway, she showed us this piece, which is beautiful by the way, and my brother was entranced with it. So I said to him . . ."

Natalie keeps talking about how Cameron came to buy it, but I can't help but sneak another peek at the man while she's droning on and on. His head is down and he's running a hand through his hair in exasperation over his sister's storytelling capabilities, and if I had to guess, it's not the first time she's so blatantly thrown him under the bus. It reminds me of the way my own brother and I do this to each other, so I smile, and with that little smile, some of the tension and embarrassment eases off his face with a welcoming smile of his own.

". . . and that's because he never got over Darth Vader being Luke's father when we were kids," Natalie finishes finally.

"Huh?" I ask.

"You know," she says, then goes on to do a pretty bad imitation of Darth Vader's infamous line of outing himself as Luke Skywalker's father.

"Oh yeah," Josie chimes in. "That moment was, like, epic!"

"Right?!" Natalie agrees enthusiastically. "What about when . . ."

With Natalie absorbing Josie's attention, Cameron tells me, "I wish I could say she's not normally like this, but she's *always* like this."

I laugh because the poor guy has this very gregarious sister who must steal the show every time he tries to get a word in edgewise. "It's okay, really," I say. "She's pretty funny, and clearly you guys are very close. My brother and I are like that when we don't want to rip each other's heads off."

He relaxes a little more and nods his head, almost as if to thank me for understanding. When Josie and Natalie are done with their discussion about whatever they were going on about, Natalie announces that it's time to get moving.

"We're supposed to be meeting up with some friends later at Rok Burger," she says. "Why don't you guys meet us there?"

Josie's face lights up, and she is about to say yes before I cut her off. "Thank you, but I don't think we'd be able to make it." And for the life of me, I don't know why I say what I say next, because I don't mean it, but it's one of those things people just say to end a conversation. "Maybe another time?"

"Yes." This from Natalie and Cameron at the same time. Then her head whips to see her brother giving her a look that only someone with a sibling could interpret as *Don't you dare say another word or I'll kill you.*

On that awkward note, Cameron and his sister say their goodbyes, leaving me with an obviously disappointed Josie.

"Why couldn't we go hang out with them later?" she asks.

Honestly, I don't really know. I feel like it was the right answer only for the sake of not being social with one of my daughter's teachers. Even if it is just a burger. But I would hate for any gossip to start and for Josie to have to deal with the fallout at school. Maybe I'm overthinking it. I probably am. Either way, I'm not changing my mind.

"Sweetie, don't you think it would be weird to hang out with your science teacher?"

She gnaws on her bottom lip for a second or two. I swear, with the amount of times she does that, it's a miracle she has any lip left to chew on.

"I guess, maybe," she says reluctantly. "But . . ."

"But what?"

"Do you think that . . ." She trails off as she looks down the street to where Cameron and his sister are still within sight. "Never mind."

I have no clue what she's thinking, but I let it go and change the subject. "*Soooo*, you sold the piece, huh?"

Josie's bright smile replaces whatever she's been mulling over. "That's right!"

She takes out the wad of bills that were stuffed in her front pocket. At first glance, the crinkly bills are an indistinguishable pile of green in the palm of her hand. Carefully, she untangles them until she counts off a total of five twenty-dollar bills.

"One hundred bucks?" I ask her in complete astonishment.

She juts out her chin proudly. "Yep. And my cut is fifty, so cough it up, Chompers."

Laughing, I hand her two twenty-dollar bills and then fish out ten dollars from change I have in my pocket. I watch as she has a mini-celebration with her newfound cash, and then I put my arm around her shoulder, bringing her in for a half hug.

"Looks like dinner's on you, kid," I say to her.

I release her and walk back to Elizabeth, who's still browsing my artwork in the back of the booth.

I can't help but double over with laughter when Josie shouts, "That's not fair!"

"You get what you get, and you don't get upset," I shout back with a huge grin.

And with that, I have the final say . . . for now, because of course I'm not going to let her pay for dinner. She earned her share fair and square, even if the owner of the sketch is someone I'm not too sure how I feel about just yet.

CHAPTER FIVE

I'm enjoying the '80s on 8 satellite radio station on the morning drive to drop Josie off at school the following week, bopping my head, singing along, appreciating the day, when she asks me something so out of the blue and unexpected, I almost veer off the road.

"Mom, are you all right?"

"Yeah, sweetie." I'm not. I'm totally lying to her right now. "Why do you ask?"

"Well." She pivots in her seat to face me. "I was just wondering why you never go out on a date. Because I've been thinking about it a lot lately and trying to remember the last time you went out with a guy."

The Cure's "Just Like Heaven" playing in the background is quickly forgotten about. She actually reaches across the console to turn the volume down to ensure that she has my undivided attention.

"I mean, you're kind of hot, you know, for a mom," she adds almost as an afterthought.

Shooting her the stink eye, I say, "Gee, thanks for that."

"Mom, I'm serious."

"I see that, kid."

I don't know what the protocol here is. I feel completely and utterly out of my depth with this topic since it's never been breached before. How do I tell her that it never was in the equation to begin with? How do I explain that dating a man, or a variety of men, wasn't in the cards for me? That it was just something that I forgot about, but that wouldn't be the truth. Because it really was a conscious decision I made a long time ago when Josie was just a baby.

"I don't really know how to answer that, Josie," I say, which isn't a lie. "I'm happy just doing what I've been doing."

I can feel her eyes boring holes into my profile, so I add, "Plus, I'm really busy."

Josie stays quiet a moment longer. "Busy doing what exactly?"

"What do you mean, 'busy doing what exactly'?"

She mumbles something unintelligible under her breath and then pivots back so that she's staring out the passenger-side window.

"What are you saying over there?" I ask.

"Nothing. Never mind."

"I don't understand why you're getting upset about this, Josie," I tell her. "I mean, it doesn't affect you in the slightest."

"See, that's where you're wrong, Mom," she says angrily. "Because I think you're using me as an excuse not to date."

What the hell? This escalated quickly.

Taking a moment to try to deflate the heaviness suddenly surrounding us, I approach a red light and turn to face Josie, who's still looking out her window.

"Hey," I say gently to her. She turns her head to look at me. "I'm happy with my life, you know that, right?"

She reluctantly nods and then says, "Are you really happy, Mom?"

In my heart I know that I couldn't have asked for a better life; a better daughter. But recently, I've felt a twinge of sadness or something else I can't quite put my finger on, which doesn't necessarily mean I'm not happy, per se. More like . . . lonely, I think.

"I am, sweetie, I swear."

"Can you promise me something?" she asks, a small smile playing at the corners of her lips.

"Of course."

By now the light is green and I accelerate the car to keep up with the bustling traffic around me. Josie smacks her lips in delight and says, "If someone asked you out, would you say yes?"

"Well, I don't know if I can answer that because I don't get asked out."

"That's because you put out the vibe that you don't want to be asked out, Mom."

Slightly stunned by her answer, I say, "How do you know all of this?"

I sneak a glance at her while I'm driving. Her eyes are shining bright and full of mischief when she says, "I pay attention. Plus, I've been watching *Gilmore Girls* on Netflix."

Laughing at her chosen source material at the same time I'm turning into her school's drop-off area, I can see from the corner of my eye that she's waiting for me to answer her. Would I go out on a date? Just asking myself that question feels awkward, so I can only imagine how the actual date would be. I did, however, tell myself that I wanted to make new strides in my social life and to be amenable to new possibilities. So maybe I should be open to this. And suddenly I'm on the same page as Josie, and a feeling of excitement rolls through me as I fully accept this option.

"You know what," I say, sounding surprised and shocked and terrified all at the same time, like I'm hopped up on the drug of life all of a sudden. And just as dramatically, I put the car in park in front of her school. "I would say yes if a man asked me out on a date."

"Awesome!"

Josie puts her hand up for a high five, and caught up in the moment, I smack the crap out of it so hard that she winces. "Oh my God, sweetie, I'm so sorry."

"It's okay, Mom," she says through a tiny laugh.

A strong tap on my driver's side window kills the mood, not to mention scares the living hell out of me. I practically jump and turn in my seat to find the parent assigned to patrol the drop-off area staring at me. Realizing I'm holding up the line of cars behind me, I push the button to slide the window down and apologize.

"Lady, you're still holding up the line. Say your good-byes and move along now."

"I was getting to that," I say to her back at this point, since she's already walking past my car to her regular spot where she oversees everything. "Jeez, somebody's in a bad mood today."

Josie kisses my cheek and bolts out the door. When I drive past the woman who patrols the through traffic and attempt to convey how sorry I am with a smile, she just shakes her head in disgust.

Well, okay then, just going to pretend that didn't happen.

I quickly put that unpleasant person out of my mind and start to go over the conversation with Josie while driving into the office. Scratch that; I totally need to go to Starbucks first and get myself an extra double shot of espresso in my coffee today after that talk.

I pull into a parking space at Starbucks a short while later. Just as my hand reaches for the front door, a semi-decent looking man steps in beside me and opens it wide with a welcoming smile.

"After you," he says.

Completely thrown off by him, I mumble a quick thank-you before ducking into the store.

Once in line, I can sense the same man who held the door open standing right behind me and staring. I glance as smoothly as possible to my side and confirm from the corner of my eye that yes, he's staring at me. I smile uncomfortably and tug some hair behind my ear in response, quickly averting my eyes. Unfortunately for me, he clears his throat and catches my line of sight again. But when he opens his mouth to say something to me, the barista calls me up and I place my order.

Saved by the barista!

Wait a second, isn't this what Josie was talking about before? Putting out a "don't approach me" vibe?

Oh my God! She's right! My almost thirteen-year-old daughter was right, and I think it's the funniest thing in the world. Further proof of this is when I start to laugh out loud like a crazy person in the middle of the Starbucks just as I'm being handed my drink.

I look like a complete loon, but I don't care. This is a huge realization for me. Because now that I'm aware of it, I can work on it and be more welcoming and open to men. Well, not open like a whorehouse open, but open to simply talking to a man and maybe a date if the man in question appeals to me.

I'm still laughing to myself when I walk by the man who had opened the door for me. He now looks so uncomfortable and is probably questioning what he saw in me to begin with, but I go right up to him and of all things . . . give him a hug.

"Lady," he says warily, "I don't know what's wrong with you, but please let go of me immediately."

Taking a step back, I wipe the tears from laughing so hard from my eyes. "I just wanted to thank you."

"Sure. Whatever, lady."

With a bounce in my step, I ignore the man's reservations and head out the door, and the smile on my face exudes how I feel at the moment: hopeful.

CHAPTER SIX

Still on a high from this morning's epiphany, I roll into work with my face still beaming with a full-wattage smile. So much so that my coworkers immediately notice. A lot of them make comments about how I seem different, while others just smile back and go back to whatever they were doing.

When I reach my desk and power up my desktop computer, I'm already thinking of how I can make myself a little more available. I don't have friends who I can call on a moment's notice, and while I don't feel bad about it, if I could change something right away, it would be that.

The only issue is with whom to start. I wouldn't know where to begin looking within what had been my close clique of friends before Josie. And honestly, the fact that they were able to let me fall to the wayside, even though I completely allowed it, kind of makes me not want to reach out and start over from scratch after so many years.

That leaves one person.

Julia.

Maybe I can get in touch with Julia and see if she'd be available for dinner sometime this weekend, seeing as how Josie has plans with her own friends. Although . . . maybe I'm being slightly presumptuous in assuming that Julia would even want to do that.

Enough excuses, Vanessa, I tell myself and pick up my desk phone in irritation to call her.

"Here's today's mail, Vanessa."

"Thanks," I say, taking the giant pile from Diana, one of my coworkers, and putting it on my desk. It looks like the Leaning Tower of Pisa, but I'm going to call Julia before I distribute it.

As I'm dialing Julia, I accidently nudge the mail, and it starts to lean a little too much to the left. I slam the phone back on the receiver, but not quickly enough to keep all the mail from toppling off my desk like a cascade of cards onto the floor by my feet.

"Do you need help?" Diana asks from her cubicle, which is just a few feet away. She stands up and darts around her desk like a gazelle. Before I know it, she's crouched down by my feet, helping me collect the mail from the floor.

"Thanks, Diana," I say sheepishly. "I should know better by now than to attempt to multitask."

She giggles and then says, "Well, it really was a huge pile of mail to begin with."

After we finish sorting the mail together, I say a quick but very heartfelt thanks to Diana before she goes back to her workstation. I'm left now with much smaller piles that are easier to distribute.

I set off dropping mail in people's in-boxes until left with my very own pile. After opening each one and rating it from important to straight in the garbage can, I'm left with one manila envelope addressed to Holt Construction that has my name listed in the address portion. Now, I may be older, and there have been many years since I've seen it firsthand, but I'll never forget this handwriting.

There are moments in your life that you bookmark for safekeeping so you can seek them out in times of need and relish the happiness of that particular memory. The memory itself may blur around the edges with time; however, it still brings feelings of elation and comfort. Sometimes, when life unexpectedly throws a giant curveball your way, as it is doing right now, and doesn't give a good goddamn about the disruption it creates, these same memories are the very things to bring you back from the depths of despair and keep you going when it feels as if there is no end in sight.

I hold the innocuous, nondescript manila envelope in my hands and turn it over and over before slicing the top open.

There is one piece of paper within the envelope in what is clearly a man's handwriting. And after reading the first sentence, the wind that had been so far blowing my sails all morning disappears with an unceremonious bang.

Dear Vanessa,

I hope this letter finds you and our baby doing well. I know it may come as a shock to you for me to reach out after all these years, but I hope you will find it in your heart to continue reading and save judgment until the very end.

First, I'd like to apologize for behaving like a reprehensible jerk. There is not a day that has gone by that I don't regret my decision to leave you and our baby behind. It has always been on my mind, and even though this is the first time I have reached out to you, it is certainly not the first time I've written this letter. There are plenty of drafts and attempts I've made over the years, but in the end, I've been nothing but a coward. It wasn't until this past year that I realized the magnitude of my decision and decided to contact you to see, if possible, if the irreparable damage I've caused you and our baby could be corrected. I don't know if you're married and if our child has a man in their life that they consider their father, but I'd like the chance for them to know their real father.

I, myself, am happily married to a very gracious woman and have recently had a blessing in the form of twin girls. These two little human beings have brought an awakening of sorts into my life. And with the help of my wife and under her advisement, she suggested that I attempt to actually mail you the letter that I've been crafting for years now and try to mend the broken bridge between us.

I realize that you must be cursing me as you read this. But I ask that you consider speaking with me at the phone number listed below so we can close this chapter in our lives and move forward for the sake of our child.

All the best,
Matthew
Phone# (305) 555-5309

All the best? All the best?!

Is he joking?

The hand holding the letter starts to shake uncontrollably with rage.

After all these years, thirteen to be exact, he has the nerve to put a letter in the mailbox and think that I'll be okay with letting him in to both of our lives? Does he honestly think with his flowery words and years-late apology, that I would allow him to be a father to Josie?

Not in a million years.

My eyes start to well up with tears as I think about the struggle that has been my life for the past thirteen years. I don't feel sorry for myself, because that's not my style. No, I'm sad for my daughter, who has no idea of the magnitude of jerk her father is. And to add to that, I'm picturing him with his perfect wife and perfect kids having the time of their lives while Josie has gone without one iota of his time for her entire life.

The day that Matthew left I had returned to the apartment we shared from my almost three-month checkup, and he was sitting on the couch. He had his head in his hands and was deep in thought. What I should have noticed was the already packed suitcase by the front door that he would later take with him, never to be seen or heard from again.

He said he had changed his mind about becoming a father. He said he didn't think he was ready. He said he wanted me to get an abortion. He said a lot of things that day. All of them splintered my heart into a million pieces and made it clear that I would be raising this child alone.

I accepted that truth eventually. It wasn't easy, but with the help of my family and then friends, I was able to move forward with the pregnancy. Six months later, Jocelyn Georgia Holt came blasting into this world, and I've never regretted a single moment of my life with her.

"Vanessa?"

I look up to find my dad standing over my workstation. He looks concerned, as I'm sure the waterproof mascara staining my cheeks is letting anyone within a mile radius know I've been crying. Quickly I stuff the letter back into the manila envelope and shove it into my purse before wiping my face with my hands.

"I was calling you, but you didn't answer." He looks at the letter sticking out of my purse and then back at me. "Is everything okay?"

"Yeah," I answer. "Everything's fine, Dad."

My dad is a very sweet man, but he's really the last person with whom I want to talk about this. So I put on a fake grin, which seems convincing enough that he seems to be okay with it and goes on to fill me in on a work situation at one of the construction sites. I nod and take notes as he speaks; all the while my brain is preoccupied with the letter in my purse.

"Got it," I say. "Is there anything else you need for me to do?"

He shakes his head. "No. Are you sure you're all right?"

"Yup, totally fine, thanks."

Reluctantly, my dad goes back to his office and closes the door behind him.

Because I *am* fine.

Or I will be since I won't be answering Matthew's letter, and I certainly won't be entertaining the thought of him meeting Josie if it's the last thing I ever do in this lifetime.

CHAPTER SEVEN

That weekend, Josie attends another sleepover at her friend Carrie's house. While she's gone, I'll be spending my time getting my frustrations out on canvas, which is the only way I know to cope when difficult situations arise in my life.

Before I head into my artist cave, I have to run a few errands. For the next couple of hours I'm going to the art supply store, followed by Home Depot, and finally ending up at the Publix around the corner from my town house.

I'm mindlessly going through the motions of testing out the quality of a particular mango when I hear my name. Turning around, I find Mr. Thomas pushing a shopping cart my way until he's standing right next to me.

"Mr. Thomas—"

"It's Cameron," he says with a smirk.

"Sorry, I keep forgetting. Well, I didn't forget that Cameron is your name. I just keep forgetting to call you that instead of Mr. Thomas."

He chuckles, and his eyes soften around the edges while he's positioning his cart around to face me dead-on. This doesn't help my nervousness, so I keep babbling a mile a minute.

"I didn't know you live around here. Do you like mangoes too?

We love them at our house. In fact, I make the best mango smoothie. It's one of my specialties."

"I can see that," he says and glances down to my shopping cart.

I've been tossing mangoes from the display into my cart the whole time I've been going off on a tangent about my ability to make smoothies. Scrambling, I grab a few mangoes at a time and put them back on the pile, only to have them start toppling down like some sick game of mango Jenga. And to my utter embarrassment, they start falling down onto the ground around my feet. The worst part is that I'm still rambling on about the different varieties of smoothies I can make using mangoes as the main ingredient.

God, how suave can I be?

Cameron bends down to where I'm kneeling on the floor of the grocery store. He smells so good this close, like if I could bottle up the sun and spray it on myself, and something else . . . hmm, maybe vanilla? Whatever it is, it's delicious. When he leans forward to help, his face is so close to mine, and I blurt out, "Did you know that your eyes are very dark, almost black like the night sky?"

Right then another mango falls on my head, keeping me from speaking out loud, which is probably a good thing if that last comment was any indication.

He tries to cover up his laughter and the ensuing awkwardness by saying, "Here, how about you pick them up and hand them to me, and then I'll pile them back up?"

In short order, I hand him one mango at a time and he stacks them strategically so that it's impossible for them to fall again. I stand and watch as he's holding the last mango and mulling over the display.

"Look," I say, pointing to what looks like an empty space on the top right of the display. "There's a spot there on the top of the pile for that last one."

"A pile is more like a heap, which sounds and looks mostly unorganized." Cameron pauses and then places the final mango on the bottom left carefully. He steps back and inspects his work. "See, by placing it just at that exact spot, the weight distribution is slightly more even, which makes it less likely for the stack to fall, even if someone takes a mango from the bottom."

I'm kind of speechless at his thought process and find myself staring at him in confusion. To most women, this process of his for stacking mangoes would be the signal to turn and run in the opposite direction. But for me, it's the complete opposite, which is a problem since I should not be turned on by my daughter's science teacher.

"I'm sorry," he says self-consciously. "Sometimes the science part of me wins out."

"Oh, don't apologize. It's fascinating that you were able to figure it out that way, because I do something similar." I turn to look at the display, tilt my head a bit while examining them, and continue. "See, I'd look at this pile of mangoes and consider the color and blush of certain mangoes and think that was too much orange on the left side and too much red on the right. I'd rearrange them so that the colors bled more into each other, almost like creating a rainbow of mangoes. And then I'd have to apologize for letting the artist in me win out yet again."

"Well then, looks like we both have an affliction."

"Looks like it," I say. "The only problem is that I actually need to buy a couple of these mangoes but don't want to ruin your scientific masterpiece."

Cameron takes a step closer, and this time I don't make a complete ass of myself and say a thing about his black-as-night eyes. I inch over as he proceeds to carefully select two mangoes that are perfectly ripe without collapsing the display again. "Here, these two ought to work for your smoothie."

51

I take them and put them in my cart. "Thank you . . . Cameron."

"You're welcome, Vanessa."

With that, he tips his head and starts to walk away, as if he had a hat to bid me adieu, like an actor from a movie in the forties . . . or maybe I'm just imagining things where he's concerned. But not even a few feet away from me, he stops pushing his cart, swings back around, and comes toward me again.

"This may seem very forward of me, and if it is, I apologize in advance. But there is a coffee shop around the corner, and I was wondering if you'd like to grab a cup with me."

I would have never guessed that that was what he was going to say. I have a million thoughts running through my brain, but first and foremost is that agreeing to meeting him, even for a simple coffee, can't be ethical with him being Josie's teacher. I'm taken aback, which must have shown on my face, because he then smiles meekly and adds, "Just as friends, to discuss the theory of mangoes, of course."

I relax a bit and surprise myself by saying yes. Albeit with my heart hammering like a hummingbird's wings, and I'm almost positive that my upper lip is sweaty from nerves. I surprise myself even further by exchanging cell phone numbers . . . just in case. Just in case of what, I'm not sure, but he asked, and I would feel like a fool if I didn't when he so readily gave me his.

"Okay, so, I'll drop off these groceries at home and meet you there in about a half hour?" I ask him.

Cameron nods. "And you'll text me if you're running late so I won't be that guy that gets stood up at the coffee shop, right?"

Laughing, I say, "Of course."

"Okay, I'll see you soon then."

He backs up his cart and turns around, leaving for good this time and leaving me wondering if I agreed to a date with my daughter's teacher or if it's really just a friendly cup of coffee.

Now I've been out of the game for quite some time, but if memory serves, this right here feels and looks like a date.

I know it's only a cup of coffee, but there's something about the way he looks at me; thoughtful and friendly, yes, but more than that. Cameron's eyes, as black as they may be, convey warmth to his every word, as if they were carefully constructed in his mind before leaving his full lips. And his lips . . . the way he licks them every so often like a nervous tic, is beyond adorable. So needless to say, I find myself in deep trouble. Because I can't deny that I am totally attracted to him.

"You're awfully quiet," Cameron says, pulling me from my straying thoughts.

I didn't even notice I had been off to la-la land.

"I'm sorry, sometimes I can be a little flighty I guess."

Why did I say that? I'm not flighty, I'm just preoccupied. Great, now he'll think that I'm a space cadet.

"I don't think you're flighty at all. In fact, you come across as anything but."

Now my curiosity has gotten the better of me. But I don't know him well enough to ask him to elaborate. I decide to try and level the playing field instead. "So, what made you decide to become a science teacher?"

He takes a drink of his coffee and puts the mug on the small table between us. He rubs the back of his neck while his face breaks into a shy smile. "If you haven't noticed, I'm kind of a nerd."

"I don't think you're a nerd at all. In fact, you come across as anything but," I say with a giggle and wink playfully at him.

Oh my God, Vanessa, get ahold of yourself and do not wink at him again.

"Touché," he says with a laugh. "Honestly, I always had a thing for scientific facts and random trivia ever since I was a little kid."

"Like what, for instance?"

He hesitates, as if telling me will divulge his inner nerd more than he thinks he already has. If possible, it makes him even more charming.

"For instance, did you know that a meteoroid can travel through the solar system at a speed of around twenty-six miles per second? Or that it's because of the sun and moon's gravity that we have high and low tides? Or that the sun is over three hundred thousand times larger than earth?"

"That's pretty impressive. I can see the appeal of that kind of stuff to a wide-eyed little boy." I take a sip of my coffee and then say, "I was never one for logical; in fact, I was the polar opposite when I was a little girl."

"I bet you were beautiful in whatever you did."

He clears his throat before saying, "I'm sorry, what I meant to say is I'm sure you were very pretty as a little girl. Dammit, that's not right either. Not to say you weren't very pretty as a little girl, not that I would know either since I didn't meet you until recently. Wait, that's not right either. What I meant to say, rather, what I *mean* to say is that you're very pretty now, just as I'm sure you were back then."

Wow, just wow. My eyes are wide as saucers as I try to take in everything that just came out of his mouth. I think . . . nah, that can't be true.

"I'm so sorry," Cameron says as he nervously fiddles with the coffee cup, turning it around and around on the table with his hands. His head is slightly lowered, but then he lifts his eyes to meet mine again and says, "I'm not very good at this, am I?"

Nope, I was right. He likes me.

The funny thing is that even though I know this isn't necessarily a good development—because the fact remains, he is Josie's teacher—I feel almost giddy from my head to my toes, like I am a teenager all over again.

"Cameron," I say gently, "I'm flattered, I really am, but . . ."

"You don't have to say it, Vanessa," he says. "I'm used to being shot down. Sometimes I wish I could catch myself before I open my mouth to speak. Actually, sometimes, I probably shouldn't speak at all."

"If it makes you feel any better, if you weren't Josie's teacher . . ." I hesitate to find the right words. "It's just not something that could happen between us. I do like you as a friend though. And I do need a friend in my life, so you can be my first new friend if you'd like."

He leans back in his chair, more relaxed than I've seen him during this entire conversation, which now that I think of it was supposed to be friendly from the get-go. But when I dig down deep inside myself, I know that I was fooling myself. The attraction was there from the moment I laid eyes on him, like a magnet pulling me to him at full force. Had I known he felt the same pull, I would have never agreed to this single cup of coffee with him. Because that's what it's going to have to be, just this one time, and then we'll go our separate ways, he back to his hot science teacher corner and me back to my parent of one his students corner.

"Vanessa, you do know that there is no rule that says a teacher cannot date one of their students' parents, right?"

"Um, come again?"

Cameron leans forward, licks his lips again, the action forcing me to wonder for the first time how they would feel against mine. Soft and plush, I bet, with maybe a hint of tenderness, yet forceful and sure so I'd know without a doubt that he wanted me as much as I wanted him.

"There isn't anything wrong with us being out like this as friends or if we were on an actual d—"

"Don't say it," I say in a panic. All this time I simply figured it was not acceptable or something to that effect. I never in a million years would have guessed it was totally okay to date one of my daughter's teachers. Which begs the question: How many other women has he tried this with? Am I only one in a long line of women he's attempted to seduce? Because that's what I think he's trying to do to me. With his supercute and sexy nerd thing, and his awkward and shy and then totally out of the blue forwardness . . . I bet he's done this before. And now I feel like a complete idiot.

"I better get going," I say and stand up. "Thank you so much for the cup of coffee, it was really nice."

Before Cameron can say anything to me, I'm already heading out the door like a torpedo, walking as fast as I can to my car to go home, which is where I should have stayed to begin with. Because there is no way in the world that I'm going to be "that woman": the one who's the sucker for a handsome face and the aw-shucks personality, along with the other countless women he's probably roped in before me.

Uh-uh, not this woman. No way!

CHAPTER EIGHT

There are two types of people in this world: those who love Halloween and those who hate it. I fall into the former . . . big-time.

Don't get me wrong, Christmas is great too, and I love celebrating it with my family every year. Who doesn't want to get presents from some jolly old man in a big red suit from the North Pole? But Halloween? Well, I fell in love with Halloween as soon as I was told that I could dress up in a costume and ask people for candy. The idea that I could become whomever I wanted for a day blew my mind. I was that kid who was already thinking of costumes by the end of the summer, and I was also that kid who had her mom sewing up until the moment I went trick-or-treating because I kept changing my mind about who or what I wanted to be.

Some of my fondest memories of Josie are of the Halloweens we've shared. Even before she was born, since I didn't know if she would be a boy or a girl, I bought unisex costumes so I would be prepared. Luckily, or really because she had no choice in the matter because I pretty much shoved it down her throat, she loves the holiday as much as I do.

I usually help out as much as I can at Josie's school events. This year, when they finally decided to take my advice and have a Halloween dance, I jumped at the opportunity to be a chaperone as well as help decorate. So for the last couple of days leading up to tonight's dance, I've left work and hightailed it to her school to work with other volunteer parents to get the decorations ready. I would be a liar if I didn't say that every time I set foot on the school's property, I'm not a little anxious about running into Cameron.

Okay, maybe a lot anxious.

I haven't seen or spoken to him since I practically sprinted out of the coffee shop a couple of weeks ago. And if I'm being honest with myself, I feel bad about that. One, because I assumed that he must be some sort of science-teacher Casanova with all the single parents of the female persuasion. And two, he was so nice, and even if nothing ever happened between us of the romantic variety, which I still am on the fence about because I bet Josie would probably freak out if it ever did, I meant what I said to him about needing a friend in my life. And he seems so genuine and kind that I think that he would be a great candidate to fill that position.

So I've come to the conclusion that if I do see him, I won't run. I'll talk to him and be civilized and try to get to a point where we can be friends. Maybe . . . we'll see. At the very least, I'll apologize for my behavior that day at the coffee shop.

I'm putting the finishing touches on my costume when I call out to Josie from my bedroom to see if she's almost ready to leave.

"Mom, that costume is awesome on you," she says when she appears in the doorway.

I turn around to find her in what I can only assume is supposed to be a costume, but I'm not sure. She's wearing a green, oversized T-shirt over tan leggings with a thin green mask like Zorro's over her eyes.

"What the hell are you supposed to be?" I ask her.

"Leonardo, I think," she says. "Oh wait, no, that's Carrie's costume. I'm Michelangelo, and Lorelei is going to be Donatello."

"You're all going to be famous Renaissance painters?"

"Mom, haven't you ever heard of the Teenage Mutant Ninja Turtles?"

"Ooooh, okay! Oh that's kind of cute," I say and go back to putting on the final piece of my costume. "Here, help me with this, please?"

Once she's done, I take a step back and inspect myself . . . I do look awesome!

I bought this Batgirl costume from a seller on Etsy about three months ago and have been dying to wear it. It's authentic Barbara Gordon circa 1960s style: black vinyl bodysuit with the yellow bat sign across the chest, matching yellow gloves with the spikes, and a yellow belt with a bat on the buckle. To finish it off, I straightened my usually wavy, long dirty-blonde hair and put a little bouffant on the top so that my bat ears look like they're sprouting from the top of my head. The only thing left is to put on my black vinyl boots, and I'm all set to patrol the streets of Gotham.

We arrive at Josie's school about a half hour later to find that Carrie and Lorelei are indeed dressed exactly as she is, and they look pretty cute when they're all together. After I get them to pose for a few pictures, which they are happy to do since I haven't met a tween yet who doesn't love an opportunity to make duck faces into the camera, I leave them to their own devices and go about chaperoning the actual dance for a while.

I'm so happy to see that a lot of the student body have shown up and look to be having a great time. A great time in separate little groups, that is. Because nobody is dancing to the music the poor deejay has been playing. When I was their age, if there was a boom box nearby, it was on, so I have no idea what to make of this.

I see one of the other moms who had been helping decorate for the last couple of days dressed as Little Bo Peep standing by herself, so I head over to where she is on the far side of the gym.

"Hey, Maria, you look great, by the way. I love your costume."

"Thanks, you too," she says. "I wish I could still wear something like that. But that last kid tore me up."

Okay, I'm just going to ignore that comment. "So are you noticing the same thing I've been noticing?"

"The no dancing, you mean?" she asks. "I think they're all afraid to be the first one out there and be made fun of."

"You think so?"

"Definitely," Maria says with a laugh. "Girl, don't you remember what it was like to be their age?"

"Of course I do, but if there was a dance at school, we danced."

Right then, the deejay of course decides to slow things down. As if this already awkward group of tweens didn't know what to do with an upbeat tempo, so he wants to take it to this level? This is a disaster.

"I'm going to go talk to the deejay. I'll be right back."

I take two steps backward on what is technically the dance floor as I'm saying this to Maria, then turn around quickly and run right into Cameron. Literally. Face-first somewhere around his collarbone. He puts his hands on my upper arms to pull me back slowly, but I keep my head down, and that's when I see what he's wearing.

It's a dark purple jacket with a green vest and a purple dress shirt underneath it. In the pocket of his suit jacket is the joker from a deck of cards. I'm almost afraid to look up, because I know that if I do, I'll be way too happy.

"Oh my God, are you okay?" he asks.

When I don't answer because I'm still staring at his Adam's apple, he takes his finger and puts it under my chin and slowly tilts my face up so I can meet his eyes, and that's when I see the green spray in his hair.

"Vanessa, are you okay?"

My suspicions are confirmed; he's dressed as the Joker. It's like costume kismet. Out of all the costumes in the world, he had to go and pick this one, and it seems to fit him to a tee. If possible, it makes him more handsome than I already thought he was. Which

I know wouldn't make sense to most women, but I'm definitely not most women.

"I'm fine, thanks, and I'm so sorry for running into you. I should really look where I'm going," I say finally. His hands fall away from my face and arm, and we stand there for a second or two in awkward silence. "I was just going to talk to the deejay about changing the music up to get these kids dancing."

He smiles warmly, his eyes doing that little crinkle at the corners thing again. "That's funny, because I was just coming over to ask you to dance."

"You can't be serious?"

"Why so serious?" he asks with a smirk.

I can't help it; I start to laugh, because that might be the most perfect comeback anyone could say to me right now.

"I figure that if the kids see someone else dancing, they'll get the idea, then follow suit. It's all quite scientific, you see."

He says this to me as he takes both my hands in his and pulls me forward a couple of steps. The next thing I know, he lets go with one hand and smoothly wraps it around my waist . . . then we're dancing before I can say no.

I glance around me to see that every single set of eyes is on us. But there is only one pair of eyes that interests me. So I keep looking until I find them over Cameron's left shoulder.

Josie is with her friends still and is watching me with her mouth agape as I slow dance in the middle of the gym with her teacher, as is the entire student body in what can only be called stunned silence. This is *sooo* bad, but I'm stuck until the song is finished because it wouldn't look too good if I ran from the dance floor. It isn't until Cameron takes me on a full rotation that I can see Josie again. But this time she has a smile on her face, which makes me breathe a sigh of relief. From the corner of my eye, I see a few kids start to trickle onto the dance floor.

"It worked," I whisper to Cameron.

He leans down to whisper in my ear. "We're practically heroes . . . even though we're sworn enemies."

"Why did you pick that costume anyway?" I ask him, still in a quiet voice.

"I don't know, I kind of just really like the look of it." He stares at me a beat, then asks, "How about you?"

"As your sworn enemy, I cannot divulge that answer." I stand on my tiptoes and quietly say, "Plus, Bruce Wayne might get jealous."

He laughs, and it isn't until that moment that I realize that the music has already changed back to an upbeat song, but we're still dancing in a slow circle, his hand wound around my waist and one of my hands lightly gripping the back of his neck. I try to put some space between us, but he stops me.

"What's wrong?"

"Cameron, we can't be dancing like this still. People will talk. Plus, my daughter is here."

I make a mental note to talk to Josie about this later tonight or tomorrow as Cameron canvasses the room to notice what I've already observed: the kids are doing their own thing; it's the parents who are still staring. Honest to God, I don't know which is worse at this point.

"Okay," he says reluctantly. "But before I let you go, can I ask you something?"

I nod.

"As I tried to tell you that day in the coffee shop, there isn't a rule in place about dating a student's parent—"

"I'm so sorry about storming off that day," I say to him abruptly. "I didn't mean to do that. I just didn't know what to think. Honestly, I still don't know what to think about it."

"It's okay." He stops moving me around in slow circles long enough to ask, "What I'm trying to get at is, well, I'm wondering if you'd think about letting me take you out to dinner sometime."

I told myself that I'd be okay with us being friends even though it would be weird knowing that we are attracted to each other. And I have been psyching myself up very recently to possibly start dating again. Even Josie was on board with the idea. But I'm not sure that this is what I had in mind. It's just too . . . I don't even know . . . maybe too close to home or something?

"Can I think about it?"

His face drops for a second, disappointment clouding his normally welcoming eyes and bright smile, making me feel terrible instantly.

"Sure. Of course," he says slightly more formally than he's spoken to me before.

With that, he lets me go and I already miss being held by him. He was a very good dancer: strong and assured, gentle, yet commanding in his leading. The best part about being so close to him was his warmth; it's like snuggling up to the best pillow ever, but only after it had been lying in the sun all day.

Now it's my turn to feel disappointed as I watch Cameron turn around and walk away from me, leaving me on the dance floor surrounded by kids dancing. It's all very surreal and like something out of a really bad eighties movie.

I feel a small tug on my right arm and turn to find Josie and her two other Renaissance Ninja Turtle Zorro mask–wearing friends bouncing from foot to foot with excitement.

"Mom, we need to talk," she says forcefully and starts pulling me off the dance floor to a small corner of the gym where the lighting is so dim that I can barely make out which one of them is which until Josie starts talking again. "Okay, so we had been planning to hook you up with Carrie's dad since her parents are divorced and that way we could be stepsisters, but this is a whole new ball game."

"Yeah," Carrie and Lorelei say at the same time.

"You like Mr. Thomas," Josie announces, and her friends nod their heads in agreement. "And he obviously likes you."

"I mean, who wouldn't? Just look at her." This is from Carrie, who inspects me up and down and then up again. "She's way hot."

"Yeah," says Lorelei.

"So we've changed the plan around so that you get together with Mr. Thomas instead," Josie goes on to say. "I mean, he's pretty cute too. Better looking than Carrie's dad. No offense."

"None taken," Carrie says, surprisingly. "He's not bad or anything, but he really needs to start working out if he wants to be a hit with the ladies. Mr. Thomas already has that part covered."

"Yeah," Lorelei adds.

I put my hands up to stop them from talking. "Girls, stop for a minute!"

They all look at me through their masks with expectant eyes. For the first time, I realize just how much Josie had been secretly hoping I'd start dating sooner rather than later, which comes as a shock even though we had discussed it recently. And for some reason, my mind goes straight to her father, Matthew, and that letter that's sitting at the bottom of my purse. Maybe it's the fact that she doesn't know her own father, and it bothers her more than she's ever let on. Or maybe she really wants me to do my own thing.

"First of all," I say to Carrie, "I've met your dad, he's very handsome, but it would be very strange to ever date him because . . . well, I've known him *and* your mother for so long and . . . let's just say he's not my type, but thanks for the offer. Secondly, Josie, are you sure you would be okay with this?"

She tilts her head to the side in confusion. "Okay with what?"

"Okay with me . . . I don't know, I guess dating Cameron?"

"Ohmygod, ohmygod, ohmygod," Carrie says in a rush of excitement. "She's already on a first name basis with him!"

"Girls! Stop, relax for a second," I say, trying to take back control of the situation. I look my daughter in the eye. "Josie, I need to know if you have even one tiny reservation about this. Because if you did, I wouldn't dare go ahead with it."

With a bright smile she says, "I am more than okay with this. I just want you to be happy more than anything, Mom."

And with those words, even if nothing were to ever happen between Cameron and me, even if I never date another man for the rest of my life, I feel relieved and assured that my daughter is more awesome than I could have hoped she could ever be.

Yeah, my daughter is a force to be reckoned with . . . and I like to think that I have a lot to do with that.

CHAPTER NINE

It's been a week since the Halloween dance, and nothing has happened. Then again, I haven't attempted any sort of contact with Cameron, so I only really have myself to blame. But he hasn't contacted me either. I can't fault him though, what with me giving mixed signals and sort of leaving him hanging about whether I would take him up on dinner.

Here's the thing . . . it's been so long since I've dated, I'm not sure if I'm supposed to call him or if I'm supposed to wait for him to call me or if I'm supposed to wait until we run into each other again or if—

Oh my God, Vanessa, I tell myself. *You're going to drive yourself crazy!*

I'm not dead though. I am aware of how much the dating world has changed since I was last out there. However, my knowledge is strictly limited to what I've read in books and seen in movies and television shows. Which isn't a very good barometer, in my humble opinion. I do not see myself being that ballsy woman who storms into his classroom in the middle of the school day and says something like, "Cameron, let's do this!"

Cameron, let's do this?

Really? Ugh, that would be more than embarrassing, and what man in his right mind would fall for that awful line?

I need to work on that part of it. Hopefully, I'll get there soon, because the word on the street, or at least from Maria, who has now become semi-friends with me, is that one of the other moms—the one who was drooling over Cameron at the Back to School Night—is setting her sights on him . . . openly. And by openly, I mean dressing scantily and showing up unannounced at the school for a quick hello, bringing him treats like cupcakes, at least on two occasions that I'm aware of, and making sure her child stays for extra-credit assignments so that she has an excuse to pop in.

Maria says that this certain mom is a word I'd rather not repeat, because I don't know the lady at all other than what I've heard, but it rhymes with bore. I'm not sure if that's true or not, but if I were a man looking to just whet my appetite, I'd consider it. Why not?

At the end of the day, everything inside of me is telling me that I need to take the next step. It's the matter of gathering up the courage to take that step that's the hardest part. I'll get there though. I can feel it.

A knock on the door as I'm preparing dinner startles me. Josie's in her bedroom upstairs, so I wipe my hands and go to answer it. I peek through the peephole to find a man on the other side I've never met before, in a pair of jeans and a button-down dress shirt. He's holding something in his hands that I can't make out clearly. Since I don't know this guy, I undo the locks but keep the link on and see immediately that it is an envelope he has in hands.

"Are you Vanessa Holt?" he asks by way of introduction.

"Um, yes. Who are you?"

He thrusts the envelope in the small space that the door allows, and it falls inside my house at my feet. "You've been served," he says and then walks away quickly.

The man is already in his car and pulling away by the time I can process all of this. I slam the door shut, lock it, and snatch up the envelope from the floor. I have no idea what this is in regards to, so I open it and take the documents out while walking back to my kitchen.

When I see the plaintiff's name, Matthew Ford, my legs start to give out on me. The breath leaves my lungs as if I've been sucker punched in the gut. Luckily, I'm right by the couch, so I sit down to try to finish reading the document.

I don't get any farther than a few more lines when I see the term "petition for paternity," and I'm having a full-on panic attack.

How dare he do this to me? To Josie? Who in the hell does he think he is that he can just waltz back in from out of the blue after thirteen years and pull this crap? Not to mention the stupid letter that, yes, I've been ignoring, but it made it seem like he was trying to be amicable about it all. But then he pulls this stunt? And how in the hell did he find out that his name doesn't appear on the birth certificate?

My head feels like it's spinning with questions and thoughts that have me on the verge of a full-on nervous breakdown. I glance at the stairs up to where Josie is none the wiser . . . yet. The threat of losing her to him terrifies me so suddenly that I start to cry, big and heavy tears run down my face as silent sobs rack my body for a few minutes.

I wipe the tears and try to compose myself. Taking a few deep breaths, in and out, again and again, until I'm semi-normal. Normal enough to take action and get up off the couch and call the one person I know I can turn to that will help me.

Digging through my purse, I find my cell phone and call Alex, who picks up on the second ring. "Hey, I was just going—"

When I hear his voice, I start to lose it again.

"Vanessa, what's wrong?"

"It's Matthew," I manage between my sobs. "He's suing me."

"I'll be right over," he says and hangs up.

In the ten or so minutes that it takes Alex to arrive, I splash my face with water and try to collect myself again. I also tend to the food that I was preparing for dinner. Josie's still in her room, completely unaware of the hurricane that has come to our front door. And I'd like to keep it that way.

Alex was my crutch during the time I was pregnant with Josie, after Matthew decided to skip out on us. And he's been the father figure in her life, the only one she's ever known. He's also the only person I ever confide in when there is something going on in my life, or Josie's for that matter, so I trust him implicitly with this.

As soon as he's in the house, he takes one look at me and wraps me in his arms.

I'm technically the big sister, but he's always acted and treated me like a precious little sister, and I find that in times like this, I'm glad that he's always been that way with me. Because I need it, especially now.

"Are you okay?" he asks with me still in his arms, and I don't answer. "Do you want me to kill him?"

This gets me to chuckle, and I pull back long enough to wipe my eyes and nose against his shirt. "Hey, I kind of like this shirt and so does my wife. It's one of her favorites, actually."

"I'm sorry. I'll buy you a new one and you can tell Julia it's my fault."

Alex turns me in his arms, then keeps me tucked to his side as he walks me to the kitchen counter. He props me carefully against the counter and then rummages through my cabinets to get a glass. After filling it with water from the sink, he promptly hands it to me. "Here, drink this and then take a breath."

I do as he says. When I'm done, I hand him the glass, and he sets it on the counter. His eyes dart to the stairs and then back at me. "Does Josie know anything about this?"

I shake my head.

"Okay, good. Don't tell her yet."

"I wasn't planning on it, Alex."

"Are you okay enough to tell me what happened?" he asks gently.

Nodding, I reach behind me and thrust the legal paperwork at Alex. As he's reading it, I say, "There was just some guy at the door. He asked if I was Vanessa Holt. I said yes and then he tossed this inside the house, and that's pretty much it."

"A process server?" he asks.

"Yeah, one of those, I guess."

He finishes reading the document and then folds it back up. "Basically it's saying that he's filing to be declared as Josie's father since his name is not listed on the birth certificate. After that, I'm not sure what the rest of it means." Alex pauses and his eyebrows furrow together in thought. "How would he know about that?"

"I don't know," I say, sounding just as confused as he does. "I've been asking myself that same question. He didn't want to be a part of our lives, so I didn't add him when Josie was born. And he never said anything about it when he wrote me so—"

"He wrote you?" Alex asks with a shocked look on his face. "When the hell did he write to you? And when were you going to tell me?"

"He wrote me a letter and sent it to Dad's office a couple weeks ago."

"I need to see this letter, Vanessa, now."

I find the letter still at the bottom of my purse and give it to Alex to read; his jaw gets tight and flexes as it sinks in. "Jesus," is all that he says after he's through.

I'm sitting on the couch while Alex paces in front of me, running his hand through his hair and not saying another word for a long moment, until I can't take it anymore.

"Alex," I say nervously. He stops pacing and looks at me. "What am I going to do? I'm really scared here. I can't lose Josie."

My brother's eyes soften and he comes over and crouches in front of me. Taking my hands in his, he says, "Vanessa, I'm not going to let that bastard take anything away from you. Ever. You have my word."

We lock eyes before he adds, "Do you believe me?"

I nod and smile and thank God that I have Alex in my corner. Honestly, I don't know what I would do were it not for him. I'm not inept and I can take care of myself; I've been doing it for a long time, but in times like these, I need someone in my corner who is going to go to bat for me, whatever the cost.

"Okay, this is what's going to happen," he announces. "First, don't say a word of this to Josie yet. Second, I'm going to call an attorney friend of mine tonight and see what he recommends your next course of action should be. If I had to guess, he will say to get a family lawyer, so I'll also ask for a recommendation. Third, you're going to go about your day and the next day, and the day after that, as if you never got this, because Josie is old enough and smart enough to pick up on anything that is bothering you."

"I'm going to have to tell her though, eventually," I say to myself more than Alex.

"Vanessa, you honestly didn't think she would go her whole life without having to know one thing about her father, did you?"

It seems like a child's answer even to my own ears when I say yes. In my heart of hearts, I knew the day would come. I never dreamed it would be today, or even tomorrow, for that matter. It was always in the back of my mind though: a deep dread, like getting several root canals all at once. But I have always been able to compartmentalize that part of my life as if it were all a bad dream so that Josie would never have to feel the shame or rejection that Matthew imparted on us all those years ago.

"I'm going to tell her, Alex, but I'm not ready yet."

Alex stands up and lets go of my hands. "Are you going to be okay if I leave now and start making some phone calls?"

"I think so," I say and stand up to hug him good-bye. "Thank you, Alex. I don't say it enough to you, but I mean it more than you'll ever know."

He pulls back and kisses me on my forehead. "You're welcome. Love you."

"Love you too, baby brother."

After Alex is gone, I do exactly as he instructed: I go back to getting dinner on the table for my daughter and me. And when we finally eat together later that evening, I try my best to hide the fear just underneath the surface that this is the calm before the actual storm that has been brought to our doorstep.

CHAPTER TEN

The next week is a complete and utter blur. From the face-to-face meeting with my new attorney, Antonia Gomez, Esquire, to the pile of work at the office, and to the planning of what is supposed to be Josie's thirteenth-birthday weekend getaway with my family, by the end of the week I'm feeling downright worn out.

Meeting with the attorney actually made me feel a whole lot better. She very calmly went over everything in the petition in detail. I expressed to her my fear that even though Matthew's been MIA all these years, that this will eventually lead to a request for visitation, or worse, custody. But after hearing the whole story, my attorney thought that a possible ruling would work out in my favor, especially since he was out of our lives before Josie was even born. So I wrote a big check as a retainer for her services with a huge smile on my face, glad to hand over the reins to her and ensure that Matthew's petition and all that it entails doesn't get any worse before it gets better.

Now it's Thursday, the night before all of us are driving up to Orlando to spend the weekend at Universal Studios, since that's what Josie asked to do for her birthday this year. She's already in bed, and I keep telling myself that I'm only tired and just need a little sleep. After I finish packing, of course, which I haven't even started yet.

The problem is I know the aches and chills and the tenderness in my throat are all the telltale signs of strep. I'm prone to strep at least once a year, and I'll be damned if it doesn't always pick the worst times to show up and ruin everything.

So I go to bed earlier than usual, telling myself that extra sleep is what my body needs, only to wake up the next morning with a full-blown fever and my throat feeling as if I had swallowed a glass full to the brim of razor blades.

"Mom, are you awake yet?" Josie asks as she raps on my bedroom door. "Don't we have to meet at Uncle Alex and Aunt Julia's house in an hour?"

I can barely lift my head off the pillow long enough to tell her to open the door. "Wait, don't come too close, I'm sick as a dog."

"Oh no! Mom, you can't be sick this weekend! It's my birthday and we've been planning this forever."

The disappointment on her face is clear as day, and I don't blame her. We've been planning this mini vacation for a few months, and if I were her, I'd be panicking too.

"I'm sorry, sweetie."

She crosses the threshold into my room and touches my forehead. "Mom, you're burning up."

"I know I am. I think I have strep throat."

"Again?"

"Yes," I say dryly. "Again, unfortunately."

I look at Josie, who is concerned for my health, yes, but also concerned that she's going to be sitting at home all weekend with a sick mother to look after. So I decide to make an executive decision. "Sweetie, can you hand me my phone from the nightstand, please?"

Dejectedly, Josie reaches over and grabs my cell phone, then hands it to me. I get my mother on the phone.

"Oh dear, Vanessa, you sound awful," she says within a second of me saying hello. "You're not planning on still going, are you?"

"No, I'm not going to be able to go," I say and glance at Josie, who's waiting for the other shoe to drop. "That's why I'm calling you. Can you swing by here on your way to Alex's house and pick up Josie? She's already packed and ready to go."

Josie screeches so loudly that whatever my mom says next is lost on me. "Mom, sorry, can you say that again?"

"Are you sure you want to stay home by yourself?" my mom asks. "I'll be worried about you, sweetheart."

"I'm sure, and I'll be fine, Mom," I say to her.

She sighs loudly on the phone. "Okay then, your father and I will be there in about twenty minutes."

"Can you let Alex and Julia know? I'm too tired to talk for too much longer."

"Of course I will," she says. "Now you go and get some rest. And make sure to eat some warm broth with toast and drink some apple juice and lots of water. And see if you can get your doctor to call in a prescription for you directly to the pharmacy."

"I will. Thanks, Mom."

I toss the phone onto my comforter and settle back in my bed. The chills pick back up then, and my teeth start rattling. Josie notices as she's still celebrating in silence on the side of my bed.

"Do you need anything before I go?"

I rattle off a list of things, which she brings to my bedroom before I hear the honk of my parents' car outside. She kisses my cheek and says a heartfelt, "Thank you, love you, and get better soon," before running out of there faster than I've ever seen her. I have to laugh and shake my head, because at least she thought to say anything before bolting. Before I forget, I call my doctor's office, which is by now so used to me having strep that they do in fact call in the script for me at the local pharmacy. But I fall asleep, or pass out is more like it, for the next few hours and never pick it up.

The next day, I still feel like a Mack truck hit me at full speed.

But I have to gather enough strength to at least make it to the pharmacy and pick up my meds. If not, I'll definitely be looking at having strep much longer than usual. Because with the antibiotics, the worst part of it is gone within a day, two days tops.

I pull myself together in the form of ratty sweatpants, a busted-up old concert T-shirt, and flip-flops, and tie my hair up in a messy bun before heading out, not even bothering to look at myself in the mirror, because really, who cares?

After I park my car in the mini strip mall parking lot where my pharmacy is located, I take a while to gather up the energy to open my car door. So I rest my head on the steering wheel for a moment. A light tapping on my driver's side window scares the living daylights out of me, and I turn to find Cameron standing outside.

Of course he would be here today of all days, when I look like this and feel like crap. And with all the drama surrounding me as of late, I haven't had a moment's peace to stop and think about him . . . us . . . whatever this is exactly.

I give a small wave before snatching up my purse and opening the door, the whole time thinking to myself that this is it. Now that he'll get a good look at what I look like, he'll go running for the hills and to the arms of that woman who's trying to bribe him with sweets and cleavage . . . or at least that's how Maria has put it.

"How are you?" he asks, shoving his hands in his cargo shorts. His black T-shirt, which fits him perfectly and makes it more than obvious to me that he's in shape, says in simple white block letters, "Gravity gets me down." He's also wearing the eyeglasses that he had on the first day I met him at the school. God, he has no idea how cute he is.

I clear my throat and sound like a frog up and died in my mouth when I answer him. "I'm doing okay."

"Oh no, you're sick. What are you doing out? You should be in bed getting plenty of rest."

"Well, I would be doing that," I manage to choke out, "but my whole family is away for the weekend for Josie's birthday, so I'm on my own until tomorrow afternoon. So that's why I look like a mess and why I'm here," I say and point to the pharmacy. "I'm picking up my meds."

Cameron smiles but doesn't say a word.

"Why are you smiling like that?" I ask finally.

"Because it seems like you need some help today."

"Not really," I say. "I live about three blocks away, so I'll be home sooner than later and back in my pajamas."

"Vanessa, I cannot in good conscience allow you to be alone in this condition."

"Cameron, I—"

"I will not take no for an answer," he says with an authoritative voice. He crosses his arms on his chest after pushing his eyeglasses up the bridge of his nose. "We're going to go inside, get your meds and any other supplies we'll need. And if you want me to run anywhere else, we'll make a list, and I'll pick up everything while you get back to resting and feeling better."

I try to protest, but he reaches out and grabs my hand and pulls me inside the pharmacy. He's so incredibly sweet to be doing all of this for me, yet I can't help but wonder if he's absolutely nuts. I mean, who goes around volunteering to babysit someone they barely know when they are sick, on a Saturday, no less? Nobody, that's who. Then again, I don't really know many people, and the people I really do know are all away. So, why not let him take care of me? If anything, it will keep me from having to do a thing, which is really what I want to be doing.

In short order, Cameron picks up my medicine along with a couple of Twix bars that he says are a necessity, cherry flavored throat lozenges, Vick's VapoRub, and last but not least, Tylenol.

"Okay," he says and ushers me outside to the parking lot. "I think we've got everything we need here."

In a whirlwind, I'm back in my car and he's following me home. And somehow, I'm totally fine with this. Because when I get home, he parks his car, follows me in, makes quick work of giving me my meds, and then commands me to change into my pajamas again and get back in bed and go to sleep.

And I do go back to bed. But the idea of Cameron hanging around in my house while I'm in my bedroom starts to eat away at me. Enough so that I know it will be impossible to fall back to sleep.

I tiptoe down the stairs and spot him on the couch in my living room, trying to figure out the remote control situation for the television.

"It's the other remote," I say to him and drag myself the rest of the way until I plop myself down on the other end of the couch. Pointing at the remote control that's still on the coffee table, I add, "That's the one that controls everything. The remote you're holding is old and doesn't work. I should just get rid of it, but I can't seem to part ways with it."

"What are you doing? You're supposed to be in bed," he says and grabs the other remote.

"I tried. Didn't take. So here I am. Entertain me."

"Entertain you?" he asks with a grin. "Hmm, did you have anything in mind?"

"You can go on to my Netflix account and maybe we can pick a TV show neither of us has watched before and marathon it. You game?"

"You're on."

Cameron and I eventually settle on *Mad Men*, me because I think Jon Hamm is supersexy, and him, well, I think he's just agreeing to watch it because I want to watch it. He presses Play on season one, episode one, and then immediately pauses the show.

"Are we quitting already?" I ask.

He laughs and stands up from the couch, reaching behind him to pull the blanket I have draped on the back of it. Then he comes to where I'm sitting in a ball and covers me with it, taking great care to tuck it in underneath my feet and pull it right up to under my chin. The whole time, his eyes are soft and his forehead is crinkled in concentration, while moving with much thought and careful consideration.

Before he goes back to his side of the couch, I say, "I think I'm good, thank you, Cameron."

He nods and goes to sit down, then presses Play and we start our little marathon . . .

I only stay awake long enough to watch the very first scene, and then I'm out like a light.

A soft nudge on my shoulder wakes me from a deep sleep. When I come to, I see that it's nighttime and the television is off, and Cameron is crouched on the floor beside me.

"Hey there," he says quietly. "How are you feeling?"

I rub my eyes and cough a little to clear my throat. "I still have the chills and I still sound like garbage."

I do, my throat is killing me, and I feel as if I could go right back to sleep for the next twelve hours.

"Is the show over? Did he jump off the building for real?" I ask him.

Cameron smiles and rubs his mouth to stifle his laugh. "No, and no. I kind of dozed off there toward the last episode I was watching."

"What time is it anyway?"

"It's around ten o'clock. I didn't want to wake you up to see if you were hungry, but since it's getting so late, I thought I'd at least let you know that I was gonna head out."

"Oh, okay," I say, and then kind of start dozing again.

"Vanessa?"

"Just give me a minute, I'll be right there and . . ." I say, trying my best to stay awake. But this sickness is kicking my ass and winning.

The next few moments are kind of a blur and kind of an out-of-body experience, because I'm not absolutely sure, but it feels as if I'm being carried up the stairs by Cameron; either that or I some-how picked up the superpower of flying when I got this case of strep throat. Even stranger is when I'm placed in my bed, then reach out to grab a fistful of Cameron's T-shirt and pull him down into my bed with me. More odd still is when I snuggle into his arms and sniff all the sunshine goodness that is his signature scent while burrow-ing into his warmth.

During the course of my broken sleep, I'm slightly aware that I'm sharing my bed with a man for the first time in many, many years. I'm cognizant of the fact that it's Cameron, which brings a smile to my face even as I'm semi-restless. And that he's holding me so close to him, like a prized treasure, and running his fingers through my hair with tenderness while my fever breaks and the dreams finally come.

CHAPTER ELEVEN

There is an erection pressed against me.

I never dreamed that this is where strep throat would lead, but there you have it.

I'm lying on my side, facing the bright sun streaming through the windows since I never closed the blinds yesterday, relishing the beauty of a gorgeous Miami Sunday morning, when I feel it for the first time behind me.

Cameron is spooning me. He has his chest and arms like a safety net around me, and it feels like a perfect bubble of comfort, from which I don't really want to move. I can sense his even breathing and a light, adorable snore that alerts me that he's sleeping soundly. But other . . . parts of him are awake.

What is the protocol here, exactly? Do I nudge him and tell him to remove it from knocking on the back door? Or do I pretend that I can't feel it and just wait for him to wake up on his own? Wait, that won't work, since he'll get out of my bed with a full-blown tent in his shorts, and that might be even more awkward. The last thing I want to do is call attention to it, even though it's doing a perfectly capable job of that all on its own.

I start to yawn, causing my rib cage to expand where Cameron's one arm is draped over me. This slight movement is enough to get him stirring, and I'm hoping he'll roll over so I can get up and out of the room and he won't be embarrassed by what's happening. Instead of rolling over, he settles in closer behind me. Then his left hand slides up the side of my body slowly until he's cupping my breast.

Okay, this is the exact opposite of what I was hoping to accomplish, and I'm frozen as still as a statue, not sure of what do next. I'm not a virgin and do not pretend to be holier-than-thou when it comes to sex, but I am in no way prepared yet to do anything with him like this.

However, my body starts to betray me when he begins to massage my breast, slowly and methodically. It's as if my mind has been hijacked by some sexual deviant, because good Lord, does that feel good. Especially when his thumb and forefinger zero in on my nipple, and he rubs it between his fingers before going right back to massaging it in his strong hand. Then it's a back and forth of massaging and tugging for a good minute.

I don't want him to stop even though I know that we should. So, thinking that he's asleep and doing a sleepwalk sex thing, I rest my head on the pillow more comfortably and close my eyes to revel in this for just a moment longer . . . and maybe even a little past that for good measure.

But then, to both my utter shock and delight, Cameron starts to press light kisses on my neck. His lips inch up slowly as he moves behind me, letting me know that he's completely awake and completely aware of what is going on between us.

My brain switches off entirely and lets him take command of my body. I mean, a few precious minutes won't kill me. Or at least that's what I tell myself when rational thought tries to infiltrate me again as my breath hitches and starts to sound more like I'm losing control of the situation.

The day old stubble on his chin rasps against my neck while Cameron continues to press kisses behind my ear in the most exquisite way, and it only adds to the sensation running through me. I grip the comforter in my hand to anchor me to this moment, to this bed, and to him a little while more. But then his hand that had been massaging my breast reaches out to capture mine. He picks it up and smoothly snakes it behind his neck, then runs his fingers down, featherlight, from wrist to shoulder, until they reach my breast again, where he picks up right where he had left off.

I'm lost in the feeling of his lips, his hands, and his body playing mine like a fine instrument. But when his hand leaves my chest and runs the length of my torso down, just past my navel and right above my pajama bottom, I begin to get slightly panicked.

My body, which had been relaxed, tightens and Cameron notices, so he stops all his movements. We stay frozen like that for a couple of seconds until he breaks the silence.

With his mouth by my ear and in a low voice, he says, "I'm sorry, I didn't mean to get carried away like that and scare you."

"You didn't scare me."

"Are you sure?"

I nod, and as my breathing returns to normal, he carefully removes my hand from behind his neck and presses a kiss to the back of it. He brings my hand down to rest on the comforter once again, but keeps his body right up against my backside.

"Okay," he says softly. He props himself up on his elbow to look down at me. "Do we want to talk about what just happened?"

Shaking my head, my cheeks turning a shade of crimson, I say, "No, I'm good, thanks. But can I ask you something?"

"Sure, go ahead."

"How did we end up in my bed?"

Cameron's face beams with a full smile and his dark eyes lighten at my question. "You don't remember me trying to leave and you pulling me into your bed with you?"

When I close my eyes, all the medicine and fever-fueled haze from the previous night comes back in a flash of moving pictures in my head. "Kind of," I say and look into his eyes. "I'm so sorry about that. You should have just left me on the couch."

"Vanessa, I—"

My cell phone buzzes from somewhere in my bedroom, interrupting him. And then I remember Josie and my entire family are due back today. My upper body jackknifes from the bed, my head darting around while I look for the phone. I find it on my dresser on the other side of the room. Leaving Cameron in the bed, I literally jump out of it and grab the phone to just miss Josie's phone call.

While I stare at it in my hand, waiting for the voice mail I'm sure she's recording, Cameron says, "Is everything all right?"

The phone buzzes with a voice mail alert, so I put up my finger to let him know I'll be a second and listen to Josie's message.

"Hi, Mom, we all hope you're feeling better. According to Uncle Alex, we're about two hours away, but Aunt Julia," she says in a deathly whisper, "says it's more like an hour and a half if he listens to her directions. Anyway, they'll be dropping me off soon and I can't wait to see you. Love you. Bye."

I turn around to see Cameron is still in my bed, his jet-black hair is a tousled mess and makes him look delectably sleepy and sexy. And for a brief second, my thoughts edge on running my fingers through it while he does things to me. But sanity prevails.

"Cameron, can we talk about this later?" I ask. "That was Josie, she's almost home. And I would really rather not have to explain this to her just yet. Especially since I was supposed to be sick."

The corner of his mouth lifts in a grin. "Well, you were sick."

"Yes, I was, but thanks to . . . you, I'm feeling much better."

He rubs his jaw as his face breaks into a beautiful smile. "You're welcome." He finally kicks the comforter off and swings his legs over the side of the bed. Slowly, he pads over to where I'm standing in front of my dresser and stops just a breath away from me. "Before I go home, since it seems we are doing things backward and I would love to spend more time with you, please say yes to my next question, okay?"

I press my lips together to keep from giggling, because that's how light and free and young he makes me feel when he says such sweet things. So I simply nod, assuming that his question is what I think it is.

"Let me take you out to dinner."

"That's not really a question," I say to him.

"No, it's not, but you already agreed by nodding your head. So, I'll be in touch to see what night works best for you, okay?"

"Okay."

With that, I follow him downstairs and open the door. He starts to walk out but hesitates, and a little bit of that shyness that he's showed me before creeps across his features. I have somehow stumbled upon a man who is willing to take things slow for me because he realizes that I need it to be that way. But I can tell that he's unsure as well, which relaxes me instantly because it's like we're on an even playing field.

"Cameron," I say to him and take his hand in mine. "I'm not spooked by what happened before, I need you to know that. I . . ."

"You what?" he asks with an expectant look in his eyes.

"I liked it."

He smiles and bends down to place a kiss on my forehead before ducking out the door; I close it behind him, my smile matching his as I lean against it.

—————

After I've showered and taken another dose of the antibiotics and eaten something, I'm already feeling so much better than I was yesterday. About an hour or so later, much sooner than Alex had projected, I hear his car pull up outside, so I press the pause button on the movie I was watching.

I'm nervous that Josie will be able to tell from the look on my face that something happened while she was gone. But maybe that will be a good way to open up a conversation about dating her teacher, even though she's already on board. I want to make double and triple sure before I move forward any more than I already have.

The front door flies open and Josie comes running in. "Mom, we had the best time!"

She gives me a big hug while I'm still on the couch, and right behind her walk in Alex, Julia, and my niece, Violet.

"Are you feeling better?" Josie asks and presses her palm across my forehead. "You're not warm anymore."

"I'm feeling much better, kid."

"Mom, I so wish you could have been there with us. Oh my God, that new Hogwarts Express train is the coolest thing ever! We have to go back so I can show you!"

Over her shoulder, I say a quick hello to Alex and Julia and ask Violet if she enjoyed herself.

Violet says as she rubs her eyes, "I had fun, Aunt Nessa, but I'm so tired."

Josie says to her, "Violet, remember you wanted me to show you something in my room?"

Violet's face lights up again and she makes a beeline to the stairs, with Josie right behind her to make sure she doesn't fall.

"Be careful," I yell and then look at my brother and his wife, who seem exhausted. "What about you guys?"

Julia comes to sit next to me and throws her feet up on the coffee table. "I need alcohol, a hot bath, and another vacation. Not necessarily in that order."

Alex sits down next to Julia. "It wasn't that bad."

"Are you kidding?" she says. "There is something to be said about those harnesses you see parents using."

"They're leashes, and no, our daughter will not be wearing one. Ever."

She crosses her arms and smiles. "Fine, then you'll chase after her the next time she runs away and straight into a gift shop and hides inside one of the clothing displays and thinks it's the funniest thing in the world."

"Violet did that?" I ask, trying not to laugh too hard.

"Yes," Julia says. She points her thumb over at Alex. "This one was busy getting a butterbeer, or so he says."

"What do you mean, 'or so he says'? I *was* getting a butterbeer, and I finished it by the time I met up with you again."

"Yeah, right," she says under her breath. "Anyway, how are you feeling? You were missed, but Josie had a really good time and as always, was impeccably behaved. Wish I could say the same about my demon child."

"I'm much better, thanks," I say. "Still a little tired, but my throat's not that sore anymore and the fever is finally gone."

It's then that Julia notices the television and tilts her head to the side at the scene at which I paused the movie.

"Um, Vanessa," she says. "Have you started stalking Harrison Ford? Do I need to be concerned?"

"No!"

"Okay, then tell me why you've asked me recently if he's hot and then I come over and boom, here you are watching *Regarding Henry*. Seems fishy."

"What the hell are you talking about?" Alex asks, propping his feet up on the coffee table as well.

"I don't want to talk about it," I say in a rush. I attempt to grab the remote to change the channel, but Julia beats me to it and snatches it up first.

"Spill. Details. Now," she commands.

I look over toward the stairs to make sure Josie isn't coming back anytime soon before filling Julia in on what's been happening with Cameron, up until he left a couple of hours ago. "So that's it.

I guess I'll be going out with him soon, and I'm a little nervous but I'm looking forward to it."

Julia looks at Alex and asks, "Did you know about this and not tell me?"

"No," he says, with his eyes closed and looking like he's about to fall asleep any second.

"Okay, so, you're nervous. That's totally normal."

"It's been a while," I say.

Julia leans forward and asks in a whisper, "How long?"

"Long."

"That long, huh?"

"Yeah," I say and rub my face with my hands. "So I'm trying to get the hang of the rules of dating and all that good stuff."

Her smile widens wickedly. "It's like baseball."

"What's like baseball?" Alex asks, popping back into the conversation.

"Sex," she says.

"How so?" he asks with a laugh.

"Well, you know like the first date is first base which equals a kiss. The second date is second base, which means it's at least a tit grab or something. Then by the third date, it's a home run and you go all the way."

"You skipped over third base, which is impossible," Alex says with a grin. "You have to step on third base; if not, you might not be waved home."

"You say toe-may-toe, I say tah-mah-toe," she says back to him.

"Why are we talking about this anyway?" he asks her.

"I'm giving sex advice to Vanessa."

Alex looks at me with his eyes wide and in shock. "Vanessa, do not listen to whatever craziness my wife just explained to you. You take all the time in the world and for the love of God, please use protection. And you," he says to Julia. "Stop being nosy."

Her laughter fills the room like a wild hyena's. "I'm not being nosy. She asked for it."

Alex stands up and goes over to where Julia is from behind the couch. He bends down and gives her an upside-down kiss on the lips, then says, "I love you, but please do not flood her brain with all this baseball sex nonsense."

He goes upstairs to check on the girls, leaving me alone with Julia, who's still laughing. "Don't listen to him," she says.

"Seriously, should I be worried that he'll expect to . . . you know?" I ask her. My mind is now in overdrive as I wonder if our next time out equals second base or is a second date, or is it technically our first date / first base situation. I feel as if we blew past first and second this morning, but we haven't even kissed yet. Oh my God, I'm going to throw up.

"Relax, Vanessa," she says. "You look like you're gonna boot. Listen, if he's half the gentleman you made him out to be, then you've got nothing to worry about."

"Okay, if you say so," I say but my mind is still racing a mile a minute. "I'm sure it will be fine."

Julia leans forward again. "Do you want to know something else?"

"What?" I answer.

"The older you get, the better the sex," she says. "It's true, especially with men. When they're young bucks all they think about is trying to hit it, and it's over pretty quick. As they get older and more mature, they realize they won't be able to hit it again and again if they don't make it worth the while for the woman. That means that they'll do just about anything to please you and make sure you . . . you know, before they . . ."

She wiggles her eyebrows like some crazy cartoon character. It occurs to me I have no idea how old Cameron is, which makes me feel like a buffoon. Because here I am going to first and maybe second base earlier today with the man, and contemplating having sex with him, and yet I don't know if he's old enough to vote.

"What's wrong now?" Julia asks. "Did I freak you out? Listen, what I said about doing just about anything doesn't mean anal or anything. I mean that could happen if that sort of thing floats your boat. And if you do anal, my friend, Sarah, says—"

"I'm not thinking about anal!" I shriek in horror. "I'm realizing that I don't know a lot about him."

"Vanessa, that's what the date part of the night is for." She pauses and takes a good long look at me. "I know it's been a long time and all, but you do remember the 'getting to know you' part of dating, right?"

"Of course I do. I'm not that stupid."

I am that stupid, apparently. But I don't dare voice that to Julia. I can still remedy this before any physical relationship goes further with Cameron the next time we see each other. My mind is drifting to all the questions I should ask him when Alex and Violet come back downstairs, with Josie trailing behind.

"I want to go home, Mommy," she says in a whimper, climbing on top of Julia.

Julia cradles her in her arms and kisses her cheeks. "Me too, sweet pea, Mommy's very tired."

"Mommy, will you naptime with me? Pretty, pretty, pretty please?"

"You don't have to ask me twice, baby."

Julia, with Violet still in her arms, says a quick good-bye, as does Alex. Before they leave though, Julia makes sure to let me know that if I need any more advice to give her a call. What with the advice she gave me today, I'm not certain that's a good idea. So I nod and say sure as politely as possible before seeing them off and out the door, leaving Josie and me alone.

Instead of telling Josie about spending time with Cameron, I end up inviting her to zone out on the couch with me for the mommy and daughter time that I've been sorely missing out on recently. Her face lights up with a beatific smile at my request, and we veg out for the rest of the day, taking turns picking what we'll watch next. As boring as that may sound, it turns out to be a perfect way to wind down this crazy weekend.

CHAPTER TWELVE

A fter a full week of radio silence from my new attorney, she calls me at work the next morning, bright and early and raring to go with a point by point breakdown of Matthew's petition in detail.

That is, until I reach a point where my inner thoughts slip out of my mouth by accident, interrupting her train of thought.

"I don't understand how Matthew could even do all of this to begin with."

"Well that's easy, Ms. Holt," my attorney calmly says. "The system is in place to protect the rights of both parents and—"

"But that's just it. He has not been a parent. He has *never* been a parent to Josie. It's only ever been me."

She blows out an exasperated breath. "Ms. Holt, I understand your frustration in the process, I really do. But it's a process. Right now, our best course of action is to file the counterpetition to his initial petition. Which as I told you via e-mail last night was in fact filed with the family court, and they have in turn already confirmed receipt."

That makes me a feel a bit better, but not much. I'm grateful that she's in my corner and even more grateful that Alex was able to find her on such short notice and procure a meeting with her immediately. I appreciate her approach and how she can break things down from the most technical legal mumbo jumbo to something

I can understand. It helps to alleviate some of the stress, but in the back of my mind, I'm already preparing for the worst.

"Then what happens?" I ask. "Worst-case scenario."

"He could very well fight your counterpetition, and then we would end up in court."

"So you mean I would have to sit there and defend all the decisions I've had to make in order to raise Josie all by myself? Then some stranger gets to decide what's best for my daughter without ever meeting her?"

"In cases where the child in question is a minor such as Josie, the presiding judge could also request to meet with the child and/or have an independent evaluation conducted on behalf of the court before ruling."

"I can't believe this," I say underneath my breath. "They could really do that?"

"Believe it, Ms. Holt." She sighs into the phone before adding, "Look, you asked for the worst-case scenario, but that doesn't mean that it will get that far. In my honest opinion, I don't believe that your ex has much to go on other than pure, unadulterated guilt for being an absentee father. I just want you to be aware of the what-ifs and be prepared for whatever happens."

"Okay."

"I'm sorry you have to go through this, Ms. Holt," she says. "But you have to trust that I am working my hardest to do what is best here for you and Josie."

"I understand that, Ms. Gomez, and I appreciate it. I just hope that it works."

"I believe it will, Ms. Holt."

After saying our good-byes, I'm left with a feeling of unease and dread as I picture Josie having to be interviewed by someone she's never met before to discuss her entire life. The more I think about this, the angrier and more frustrated I get over the entire legal process. I just have to trust my attorney to make the correct decisions and have faith in her belief that it will all work in my favor in the end.

I've also decided that I'm not going to tell my parents just yet about any of this mess with Matthew. I know that it will only add an unnecessary stress into their lives if I do. That's not completely true. There is a part of me that feels like somewhat of a disappointment to them. I mean, I had a child right out of college *and* out of wedlock. Even though I know they don't have an issue with any of it since they've been so supportive of me, I don't want to have to tell them about a problem that involves Matthew . . . again. So, as of right now, the only person who knows what's going on is Alex. Who, thank God, has been able to keep things quiet about it to date. However, he now thinks it's time to tell Josie, and I will . . . I just can't seem to pick the perfect time to do that.

When my cell phone starts to ring in my hands, it shakes me out of my depressing and futile thoughts. Looking at the screen, I see that it's Cameron calling me, and it's a welcome distraction.

"Hello, Cameron."

"You didn't call me Mr. Thomas right off the bat. I'm impressed and honored."

"You should be."

"How is your day going?" he asks.

I'm not about to start unloading on him all the drama surrounding me right now so I take the safe route. "Fine. How about yours?"

"Funny you should ask, because I'm good. Great, actually."

"What's so great about it?" I ask.

"Well I've been sitting here planning our date," he says with an air of excitement in his voice.

This throws me for a loop. Even though we agreed to see each other this weekend for what would be our first official date, I didn't think he would be mapping it out so seriously and with such gusto.

"What did you have planned, exactly?"

He takes a quick breath and then lets loose all the things he has been planning for us to do on Saturday, beginning with a wine tasting and ending with a laser light show at the planetarium. In the middle of those things, he wants to squeeze in a trip to Bayside to take a boat ride around Star Island and of course dinner somewhere close to the beach.

"Cameron," I say hesitantly. "Don't take this the wrong way, but I'd like to keep things simple."

"Um, I'm sorry, was I going off the deep end already?"

"No, it's sweet of you, really, to want to make sure I'll have a good time. But I promise, I'll have a good time no matter what we do together."

"Okay," he says, sounding slightly unsure. Now I feel terrible that I made him second-guess himself.

"Cameron, I hope you realize that more than anything, I really would like to get to know you better, and I think keeping things simple is the best way to do that."

I can hear the relief in his voice instantly. "I'd like that too, Vanessa, very much."

"Good." And now I'm the one who feels more than relieved.

"Good," he agrees. "So I'll pick you up at six o'clock on Saturday night then?"

"I'm looking forward to it."

When I wake up on Saturday morning, Josie is already downstairs on the couch, reading a book. I can feel her ever-observant eyes tracking my every movement as I turn on the pot of coffee in the kitchen and wait impatiently for it to brew. Once I've poured myself a cup, I sit on the other couch across from her.

We stay silent for a moment or two until she says, "So tonight's the night?"

"Looks that way."

I told Josie about going out to dinner with Cameron, and she was very happy for me. Today, as I blow on my coffee to cool it down a little, she seems off, as if there's something bugging her. Naturally, being the semi-pessimistic person that I am, I'm guessing that she's not as okay as she thought she was about her mom dating one of her teachers.

Gingerly, I put my still-full mug on the coffee table between us. "You know, Josie, it's normal for you to be upset about this. And if you say the word, I'll call Cameron right now and call it all off."

Josie drops the book she had been reading onto her lap. Her eyes scrunch together in confusion, and she's about to say something to me, but I put my hand up to stop her.

"Because you know, kid, I think we've been doing a fine job with just the two of us up until now. And I would hate for you to feel uncomfortable in the slightest with me dating. Or I should say, dating your teacher, specifically, which is kind of weird, but—"

"Mom!"

"Yes?"

"Are you crazy?" she asks and doesn't let me answer. "Of course I'm okay with this. I was only asking if tonight was the night because I wanted to know what you were going to wear and if you needed any help with picking out an outfit."

"Oh."

Josie offering to help me releases a little of the stress I'd been holding on to leading up to tonight. Having two parents who are still happily married some thirty plus years now and a brother who went the traditional route with his love life, kind of, I've always felt bad about not having a so-called normal home life for Josie. So to hear her be so accepting and wanting to help me today, especially with me being so nervous about it all, is like a weight off of my shoulders.

My eyes start to water immediately.

"Mom, it's not a big deal, it's just clothes."

Wiping my eyes with the ends of my T-shirt, I smile at her reaction. Then I try to get control of myself before I really start to cry, over of all things, a date.

"Seriously, Mom."

"Yeah, I know," I say. "So clothes. Right. I was thinking a pair of jeans and, I don't know, a top or something, and some sandals."

Josie looks at me as if two heads sprouted on each of my shoulders while I was talking.

"Is that not good?" I ask sheepishly.

Her face then morphs into a sly grin. "Let's go to the mall. But first, I'm going to call someone for help."

"We don't have to go to the mall, Josie. I have plenty of clothes here already."

"Mom, your clothes all have stains on them from painting and drawing. And the 'nice' clothes you think you have aren't that nice. So a couple of new outfits aren't going to kill you."

While she's talking, she has her cell phone out and is pressing buttons maniacally.

"Who are you texting?" I ask.

"Aunt Julia," she says. "She already texted back that she'll meet us at Dadeland in about an hour and to bring Spanx." She looks up at me in confusion. "Do you know what that means?"

"I don't have any." Josie presses more buttons on her phone. "What are you texting her now?"

"That it's a code red situation since you don't even own Spanx."

"It's not a code red situation, thank you very much," I mumble to myself. Her phone buzzes immediately. "What's she saying now?"

"She texted back that she'll meet us in thirty minutes instead and not to be late." Josie stands up from the couch and starts walking past me. She stops, bends down, and gives me a big hug, then says, "Make that coffee to go, Mom. We've got some serious shopping to do."

CHAPTER THIRTEEN

Several hours later, I'm standing in front of a full-length mirror in my bedroom, not quite sure if this is what I had in mind by keeping it simple.

I'm wearing a brand-new pair of boyfriend jeans with the cuffs rolled up to showcase an also new pair of black, ankle-strap heels. I have on a plain white, thin, V-neck T-shirt covered by a tailored black blazer that fits me perfectly and lands just at the beginning of my hips.

After a few discussions with my stylists, Julia and Josie, they decided it would be best if I wore my hair down and in its naturally wavy state. They insisted that I wear a pair of gold hoop earrings. And Julia, who brought with her some items from her own closet, let me borrow a leopard-print, fold-over clutch that has a giant gold zipper. This is because I need to accentuate the gold from the earrings and the buckles on my heels, or that's what she said before giving me a once-over and saying her job was done before leaving me alone with Josie about an hour ago.

I'm not a big makeup person, so I put on the bare minimum: light powder, a little blush, mascara, and a rose-tinted lip gloss.

Josie stands behind me in the mirror, inspecting her work. "Mom, you look beautiful! Mr. Thomas is going to flip out!"

"You think so?"

She nods her head like a crazy person while a smile spreads across her face.

"Grandma will be here soon," she says with glee while checking her phone for the millionth time. "So that means Mr. Thomas will be here soon to pick you up."

When I called my mother earlier in the week to babysit Josie for me tonight, at first she said she couldn't do it because my parents had plans of their own. Then she asked where I was going. And when she found out . . . she just about had a heart attack and immediately canceled her plans.

When my mom arrives, she takes one look at me all dressed up and bursts into tears.

"Mom, Jesus, it's only a date for crying out loud."

"I know, I know," she says. "Your father and I are so excited for you. We have been praying for years for this moment."

"Okay, Mom," I say to her and give her a hug. "Get it together. You can do this."

"Oh no, I don't want to ruin your outfit, Vanessa! Let me go!"

She practically shoves me off of her. "Now let me see this masterpiece."

Josie chimes in, "Aunt Julia and I picked it all out, Grandma."

"And you both did a beautiful job, sweetheart."

A knock on the door breaks up the pep talk / fashion critique. I glance at my wristwatch to see that Cameron, if anything, is extremely punctual. Call me crazy, but I love that in people, since there is nothing worse than saying you're going to be somewhere only to be late, or worse, really, really early. But he's right on time.

Point one for Cameron.

My mother and Josie follow me to the door like lemmings. I'm already nervous and feel like I've swallowed a hummingbird that's nested in my belly and is flapping its wings around in there. But then

99

both my mom and my daughter walking right behind me as I go to open the door only makes the nerves worse.

In a whisper-yell, I say to them both, "Back it up! Go to the kitchen or something."

With dejected looks, they run off to the kitchen so I can finally open the door.

What I'm greeted with is head-to-toe perfection . . . and I hate to be *that* woman, but my heart may have literally skipped a beat or two at the sight of him. He's wearing a pair of dark jeans and an untucked black button-down dress shirt. His jet-black hair looks as if he just ran his hands through it with some hair product, styled but not too styled. And those dead-of-night eyes of his that I really like are highlighted by his wire-rimmed eyeglasses. He's finished it all off with a pair of classic black Converse sneakers.

"Vanessa, you look stunning," he says finally, after a moment or two of us just staring at each other.

"Thank you. You're not so bad yourself."

He does that licking of his lips thing he does, which only serves to remind me that I'm probably going to be kissing those very lips later tonight. I might as well have dropped a bomb right then and there. Because the rest of the night, all I will be doing is imagining when, where, and how it will be to finally feel his mouth against mine.

"Vanessa?" he asks.

"Oh, I'm sorry, please come in while I get my purse."

Stop thinking about his lips, stop thinking about his lips, stop thinking about his lips, I say to myself on repeat as I wave him inside my house.

This ends up being a huge mistake, because of my mother. Josie, she knows him. But my mother . . . doesn't. So what begins as an introduction ends up being a litany of questions like these: "Where did you grow up? Are your parents still married? Do you have siblings? What is your driver's license number?"

"Mom! What the hell?" I shout, then turn to Cameron. "I'm so sorry. You do *not* have to answer that last question."

I glare at my mother, who is pretending to look like she meant no harm. Josie is right beside her, trying her hardest not to laugh and failing miserably.

To Cameron's credit, he grins and answers all of her questions, one by one. "I grew up in Port St. Lucie, my parents are indeed still married, and I have a big sister named Natalie. As for my driver's license number, I don't know it off of the top of my head but it is in my wallet, which is in my car. So if you like, I can go get it for you."

"No, you will not," I say with an uncomfortable smile. "Okay," I say to Josie. "You be good for your grandmother. And you," I direct to my mother. "You be good for Josie."

They both laugh as I grab ahold of Cameron's hand and lead him toward the door. "I'll be home by . . ." I turn to him with a question on my face since I really don't know what time I'll be home, because I don't even know where we're going.

"Oh, right," he says. "I'll have her home before midnight. Scout's honor."

"Were you a Boy Scout too?" my mom asks in delight.

"Mooom!" I say through clenched teeth and open the door to leave. "I'll see you both later. Actually, kid, I'll see you tomorrow morning, since you'll already be in bed. So good night, love you."

"Love you too," Josie says. "Have a great time."

I close the door behind me and breathe a sigh of relief for escaping that awkward situation sooner rather than later. Feeling a light squeeze, I realize we're still holding hands. He places a soft kiss on the back of my hand just as he did the morning he woke up in my bed with me. He doesn't say a word, but he doesn't need to. Because with that one gesture, I feel the tension and nervousness of what's ahead recede a little. His eyes though, they ask an unspoken question of me: *Do you trust me?*

I do, I answer him silently.

And then we're off.

"How did you find this place?" I whisper as the hostess walks us to our table. He doesn't answer and only grins in response.

Cameron's hand is on my lower back; the contact, as light and brief as it is, feels exhilarating. He leads me gently, following the hostess through a canopy strung with white lights that leads to an outdoor dining patio. We finally reach our table, and he holds my seat out for me before sitting down across from me. Before leaving us alone, the hostess lets us know that our server will be with us shortly.

"You promise you won't laugh?"

Now my curiosity is piqued. "I promise."

"I looked up best restaurants for a first date in South Miami, and this one was on the list. I figure if it made such a specific list, it had to be good."

"Why would you think I would laugh at that?" I ask. "I think that's very thoughtful and sweet of you."

He shrugs and relaxes a little bit in his seat. "I'm glad you like it."

"It" is Peacock Garden Café in Coconut Grove. I've heard of it, of course, but have never been here before. And it's quite lovely. Orchids and plant life surround us, so it feels a bit removed from the hustle and bustle of this area, but not so far that you can't feel the air buzzing with excitement just a stone's throw away. The patio dining area is pretty full tonight, and it's only about seven o'clock. Our table is nestled in the far corner of the patio, giving us some privacy, which is perfect. Most people can spot that first-date couple a mile away, and the last thing I would want is for people to stare at us with the "Oh, how cute are they? They're on their first date!" looks on their faces.

After the waiter takes our drink order for the white wine sangria—the house specialty—I lean forward and rest my elbows on the table.

"So."

He leans forward and rests his elbows on the table too and says, "So tell me about yourself."

"Like what?"

"I don't know." He chuckles and shakes his head. "I don't know why I just said that, because that's not true either. I want to know everything about you, so start at the beginning if you like."

Just then, the waiter brings over our drinks and I take a small sip before answering. "That's a lot of history. Why don't I give you the abbreviated version instead?"

"By all means."

"I was born and raised in Miami. I've lived here all my life except for when I went to college in Tallahassee on an art scholarship."

"That's impressive," he interjects.

"Where did you go to college?"

"Michigan State University."

"That's pretty impressive too. How did you end up there from Port St. Lucie, then back down here in Miami?"

"I applied to a lot of northern schools so I could finally experience a true winter. They had a really good program for my major, so I went with it. But those winters really took their toll on me and I missed the warm weather. So I completed my student internship back home near Port St. Lucie before I graduated. But after that, I wanted a change of pace *and* scenery, so I applied to teach in South Florida. And that's how I ended up teaching full-time at Josie's school for the past six years."

"Why did you pick teaching?"

His face lights up and the corners of his lips turn up in a small smile. "Do you remember how I told you about all those science facts I was obsessed with as a little boy?"

I nod while taking another sip of my drink.

"Well, it wasn't until ninth grade that I found that I could marry the two, so to speak. My science teacher that year made learning fun, instead of the dull, boring lessons my previous science teachers had given. She showed me that teaching could make a difference in someone's life. It inspired me, and ultimately it stayed with me and made me want to pass that on to other kids. I get a real kick out of seeing a kid struggling with a lesson and not being able to get it right away. But when they do . . . I can almost see the lightbulb switching on for them, and it's the best feeling in the world when that happens. Because I've reached them somehow and they are potentially experiencing the same inspiration I felt when I was their age. And who knows? Maybe that one little difference in their lives is enough to get them thinking of being a teacher too . . . or something else."

"That's beautiful, Cameron," I say, genuinely impressed.

"How did you become an artist?"

"I wouldn't say I'm much of an artist, really. I'm more part-time." I lean back to let the waiter put our appetizer of crab cakes in between us. "Actually, I'm more part-part-time artist at this point."

"You shouldn't do that."

"What?" I ask.

"You shouldn't sell yourself short or try to downplay what you were obviously born to do. You are an artist. And you're very talented," he says. "That piece I bought at the art fair last month . . . it's amazing."

"Thank you," I say.

I can't bring myself to say much else after his compliment. It was genuine and heartfelt, and I can tell that he meant every single word. And if I'm being honest with myself, he's right. I shouldn't downplay how much time I spend doing what I love to do. Even if I don't have much time to devote to it.

"And to answer your question, I always had a thing for drawing and sketching since as far back as I can remember. My mom, you know, the crazy lady you met earlier tonight?"

"She wasn't that bad," he says with a laugh. "She's only looking out for you, as well she should."

"Well, she put me in art classes starting at four years old, as soon as she saw that I would draw for hours on end—all day sometimes. It was just always something I could do. My mom tells me that when I was three years old, I was already coloring inside the lines like a pro and doing self-portraits. She would also take my brother and me to museums and gallery exhibits, and both of us absorbed the beauty all around us like sponges."

"Oh, so your brother's an artist too, then?"

"No, not quite. But he owns a gallery down in South Beach."

We continue this easy back and forth of getting to know the basic history of each other throughout the course of the meal. And it feels completely comfortable and easy to talk with him. I don't know if it's the setting, or simply that it's just nice to talk to him, specifically. But whatever it is, it makes the dinner go by so much faster than expected, and before I know it, it's almost over.

Then, of course, the dreaded questions about Josie's father come. I knew they would; I'm not a fool. But I was kind of hoping that I wouldn't have to field them tonight, what with all that is going on with Matthew right now. So I only give him the basics: that Josie's father was my boyfriend for a few years, we lived together, and then he decided he didn't want to be a father at such a young age. Technically, we were both in our very early twenties, but whatever, it works for the purpose of telling Cameron the background on Josie's father without giving away too much. But what I don't tell him about is the petition for paternity.

"So he's never met Josie?" Cameron asks.

"No, never."

"I'm sorry seems like such a trivial thing to say to that, but I am . . . I'm very sorry that happened to you and Josie."

"Thank you, but you don't have to be sorry. Josie and I are very happy, and she's kind of amazing, so I've been very lucky."

He raises his almost empty glass of white wine sangria, so I lift mine to clink against his. "To you and Josie then."

I take a quick sip, then ask him something that's been at the very back of my mind for a few days. "Have you ever dated someone with kids before?"

"No," he says with a genuine smile. "Have you?"

Caught off guard, I point to myself and try not to laugh. "Me? I haven't dated anyone in years, so no."

"Then we're in the same boat," he says.

I lean forward and whisper, "Does that worry you?"

He leans forward, his face coming so close to mine across the table that if I moved an inch more we'd bump noses. It's not uncomfortable though; it's just . . . *really* close and feels intimate and reminds me of the day he woke up in my bed. Then that reminds me of all the things that happened that morning between us that we haven't even touched base on yet.

"No," he answers just as quietly as me.

The waiter brings Cameron's copy of the check then and breaks the moment. He wishes us a good night as we leave the restaurant. We head out into the busy streets of Coconut Grove for a walk around the area, just taking in the sights and talking and talking and talking. And it feels so damn good to go out and talk with someone other than a family member. It's refreshing and freeing, and Cameron puts me at such ease that I don't feel off-kilter or pressured or uncomfortable in the slightest.

Then it's time for him to take me home. The entire drive back to my house is filled with dread over what is going to come next. Because the idea of kissing Cameron is something I've thought about already . . . often and vividly. And I want to, I really do. But I'm so out of practice that I feel as if I might disappoint him. My God, that would be *sooo* embarrassing.

So when we pull up to my town house, he walks me to my door in complete silence. Me, because I'm wondering when he'll strike. Him, probably wondering if I'll even let him.

"I had such a good time, Cameron." We're standing at my front door, and I feel as if I've been transported back to my high school years, when I was way more savvy about this kind of stuff even if I was technically less experienced. "Thank you for dinner, it was absolutely delicious. And that restaurant you picked was perfect."

I keep rambling on while his eyes dart from my eyes to my mouth and back again. Then, without a word, he takes a step forward, and then another, until my back is against the front door and I shut up.

I watch in anticipation as he reaches out to hold my face in his hands, stroking my cheeks with the pads of his thumbs lightly. "You are so beautiful, did you know that?" he asks me in such a low voice, I barely register the question.

But with a slight shake of my head, I answer him, because I can't form a coherent sentence. He moves forward then, his body pressing against mine in all the right places and causing every single nerve ending to light up like fireworks at the same time inside of me.

He bends his head down closer and I feel his lips brush against mine when he asks, "Is it okay if I kiss you now?"

Licking my lips in response, I drop the clutch I was holding on the front step and grab his wrists in preparation.

When he finally presses his mouth fully against mine a second later, it's everything I thought it would be and more. His lips feel lush, hesitant yet assured, but the most surprising part is the pure hunger coming off of him and vice versa. But when his tongue darts out to taste mine, I lose myself in the moment and in him. It's perfect; soft and slow, and a tantalizing preview of what he could do to me were this not just a first kiss.

I lose track of how long we stand there kissing, but when it's over, my heart is still racing and wanting so much more from him.

"When can I see you again?" he asks, then presses another quick kiss to my lips. "I need to see you again."

My eyes are still closed, waiting and hoping for more. When it doesn't come, I'm surprised at my disappointment. So I open my eyes, only to find his dark ones fixated on mine in anticipation of my answer.

"Soon," is all I'm able to say.

Cameron offers a shy smile, letting a little of that unsure and nervous side of him come out. It's reassuring and sexy and makes me fall even more for him.

"Next weekend?" he asks.

His lips place a tender kiss on the corner of my mouth, then move to my jaw, where he presses kiss after kiss, softly and strategically, waiting for my answer. My head lolls back and my eyes close once more, enjoying the moment and wanting to prolong it as much as possible before the spell is broken again.

When he stops this time, and with my eyes still closed, I say, slightly out of breath, "Yes, definitely next weekend."

"Good," he says with a light chuckle. "Next weekend it is."

Once I open my eyes again, he's dropping his hands from my face and taking a step back. I miss him already, and it's not just the intimacy or the closeness of what happened; it's *him*, which scares me. I don't want to fall any more for him than I already have in the short time I've known him, but I see myself doing exactly that with each word that comes out of his mouth, with each tender gesture, and when he reveals that shy and reserved and sometimes very confident and sexy side of him. It's a lethal combination.

Cameron bends down to pick up the clutch I carelessly dropped on the concrete steps and then hands it to me with a grin while taking the last few steps until he's on the concrete walk to his car. He turns around once more to look at me, still standing against the front door. There are no words shared between us, only a silent question again held within his eyes.

Do you still trust me?

My genuinely satisfied smile is the answer . . . *yes.*

CHAPTER FOURTEEN

A quick knock on my bedroom door wakes me from a very deep sleep. Then the door swings open and Josie comes running in. She practically jumps into my bed and burrows underneath my covers.

With her head on the opposite pillow, her excited little face is the very first thing I see once my eyes come into focus.

"Good morning, kid," I say to her and rub my eyes.

"How was it? Was he romantic like in the movies and sweep you off of your feet?" she asks in a rush.

"He was . . ."

"Did he treat you well?" she asks so suddenly and earnestly that I'm taken aback by her question.

"Why do you ask that?"

"Uncle Alex always says to me that any boy that asks me for a date—" She stops and then adds, "Relax, Mom, when I'm older, of course. Anyway, that any boy that asks me out must treat me well, be very respectful of me, be a very good listener, and that I should never sell myself short. And that any boy who doesn't do any of those things, I should kick him to the curb."

"Well, I think that Uncle Alex would probably want to kill this boy even if he did all those things. The poor imaginary little guy," I add as an afterthought.

We both laugh but it's true. I feel so sorry for any boy in Josie's future who will dare to ask her out. Because, having been the victim of a broken heart by her father and other boys before him, I'm fully aware of what they are like and capable of. Add to that her uncle's protective streak that borders on psycho, and he's in for a hard time regardless of if he was the sweetest, most perfectly behaved boy to her.

"To answer your question—"

"Questions," Josie says, correcting me.

"Right, right, sorry. Well, to answer your questions, yes, he treated me well, and I guess it was romantic."

"Did you kiss him?"

"Josie! That's kind of personal, don't you think?"

"Mom," she says with a lift of her eyebrow. "Give me a break, you either kissed him or you didn't. Which is it?"

I roll over and stretch my arms over my head. Josie comes closer and brings her face right up to mine where I'm trying to keep the coy smile from breaking across my face.

"Aha! You totally kissed him!"

"A lady doesn't kiss and tell, remember that sound piece of advice, by the way," I say to her and get out of bed. "So what do you want to do today? And please do not say the mall, because I've had my fill of the mall yesterday to last me a lifetime."

Moving around my room, I grab my robe off the back of my closet door absentmindedly and put it on. Noticing that Josie isn't saying a word, I turn around to find her still on my bed and deep in thought.

"Sweetie, what's wrong?"

"What happens if it doesn't work out? Or what happens if it does and you guys end up falling in love and getting married?"

Whoa, whoa, whoa, that's kind of jumping the gun, and I'm somewhat surprised that she's even thinking in those terms when this was only the first date. The first date of many, I secretly hope to myself, because I really and truly like Cameron a lot, but the thought of marriage isn't even a speck on the clouds of thoughts running through my mind where he's concerned.

I sit down beside her and take her hand in mine. "Josie, first of all, if it doesn't work out between Cameron and me, so be it. Things happen in relationships all the time. You'll see for yourself when you get older. Sometimes even the best of intentions doesn't necessarily lead to the best situation for everyone involved. And secondly, if—and that is such a big if, sweetie, that I don't even know where to start—if ever this became something more than it is, I wouldn't make any kind of decision without consulting you first. Because it's always been me and you, kid . . . and that's the way it will always be to me."

Josie's smile washes away the worry that was clouding her features, and I feel better about her knowing this. I reach out and brush some of her crazy, bedhead blonde hair away from her forehead and tuck it behind her ear.

Holding her chin in my hand, I search her blue eyes to ensure that she's okay. Once I feel assured that all is well between us again, I ask, "How about some pancakes and then a matinee somewhere, wherever you want and whatever movie you want to see. What do you say?"

"Okay."

While Josie and I are at the movies later that Sunday afternoon, I receive an unexpected call from my attorney. I excuse myself to go to the lobby.

"Ms. Holt," she says. "I'm sorry to bother you on a Sunday, but I thought you'd like to know immediately as soon as something came up."

I'm barely holding on, because for an attorney to call you on a Sunday . . . that cannot be a good development. "No, that's quite all right, Ms. Gomez. Please, go ahead."

"Okay, well, your ex has made a specific request, and if you agree, he'd be willing to drop the petition for paternity he's filed against you."

"What does he want, exactly?"

There is a distinct pause from my attorney, one that speaks volumes and says to me already without her voicing it that I'm not going to like it one bit.

"He will drop the petition if you agree to let him meet Josie in person, supervised, of course."

My head feels like it's spinning already, trying to picture this meeting between Matthew and Josie. "Wait, I'm confused."

"What's there to be confused about? He's willing to drop the petition if you agree to this condition."

"I'm sorry, what I mean is he just wants to meet her one time? That's it? And then it's all over?"

"Well . . ."

We let that settle over the phone between us because I knew it! I knew there had to be more to it than just a simple meeting.

"Tell me what he wants," I demand. "All of it."

"Well, the truth is that's all he's requesting at the moment. But if I had to guess what his next move would be if you do agree to this, it's that he'll then request some sort of visitation schedule. Then again, if we end up going to court and the judge rules in his favor, that could end up happening anyway. Ms. Holt, this could drag on and on and end up costing you a lot of money. However, if you still do not want to move forward with any of this, simply say the word, and I'll give our response to his attorney."

"I need to think," I say to myself more than to the attorney.

"Of course, I wouldn't expect you to have an answer immediately," she says. "How about you give me a call tomorrow afternoon, after you've had a day to think about it?"

"Yes, that's fine. I'll do that. Thank you."

As if on autopilot, I walk back into the movie theater and sit beside Josie. I don't know what the hell happens in the rest of the film, and I don't care either. My mind is so frantic with worry over which is the best decision for me, for Josie, that I can't concentrate.

Even after the movie when we get back home, I'm a basket case. The one prevailing thought is that I can't trust Matthew with Josie because I don't want her to get hurt by him again. Granted, the first time he hurt her was when he walked out before she came into this world, but that hurt lasts a lifetime: enough so that I couldn't bear it if I had to watch her go through it now, at such an important time in her life.

Later that evening, I put away the dinner dishes and Josie goes to her room for the night and me to mine, I decide to call Alex and ask for his advice.

"I don't know, Vanessa," he says after I've given him the rundown of my options. "A part of me thinks screw him and go through the courts. But another part of me is on the fence *because* of the courts."

"How do you mean?" I ask.

"Well, think about it," he says matter-of-factly. "Going through the courts guarantees that he will be heard, which with his history may not look favorably upon him, but you never know with these things. It makes me nervous."

"Yeah, it makes me nervous too. But I don't want him to think he can just waltz back into Josie's life and pretend to be the father he never has been to her all these years. He can't get away with that, Alex!"

"I know, Vanessa," he says calmly. "What is your first instinct?"

"What do you mean?"

"I mean, in regards to one way or the other. If a gun is to your head and you have to choose—and you do, because the attorney is expecting an answer tomorrow."

I don't even think twice, I know my answer. "I still want to fight the petition for paternity."

"Then there's your answer, Vanessa."

The next day I phone my attorney and tell her my decision. She doesn't say yea or nay or voice anything on the matter, other than to let me know that she'll take care of it. This is exactly what I wanted to hear, and I put Matthew, for the time being, out of sight and out of mind.

CHAPTER FIFTEEN

My buzzing phone wakes me up bright and early the next morning. My alarm hasn't even gone off yet, so naturally, I think it's an emergency.

I don't look at whose calling and swipe the screen to answer it frantically. "Hello?!"

"I'm sorry, did I wake you?" Cameron says.

Relief washes over me once I realize that it's not some cataclysmic event. I fall back onto the pillows with a sigh but am completely confused why he's calling me this early, like ridiculously early, like inhuman early. "You did wake me up, yes."

"I'm sorry."

"You said that already," I say with a small laugh. I check the clock on my nightstand and see it's almost five o'clock in the morning, when my alarm is supposed to go off. Leaning over, I switch it off and prop myself up on the pillows. "And it's okay, my alarm was going to ring in about five minutes anyway."

"I remember you told me that you like to exercise really early during the week, I do as well, and . . ."

"And?" I ask, smiling into the phone.

"And I was thinking about you when I woke up this morning so I was hoping to catch you before your day got too busy."

"Are you always this nice?" I ask, genuinely curious. Because if he keeps this up, I may be spoiled rotten in whatever future we may have together.

His soft chuckle precedes his answer. "I don't know about that. I can be mean and get angry just like anyone else."

"Oh, yeah? Prove it."

"Well, just the other day . . . you know what, never mind."

"No, no, no. Now you're going to have to tell me."

He sighs into the phone. "I was going to say that a few weeks ago, I went to a comic book store and they had recently sold a copy of an old comic book I have been searching for, for a while, to another collector. Needless to say, I was a little upset."

Even he's laughing at the ridiculousness of that statement. But even as ridiculous and trivial as it sounds, I still don't blame him. I mean, some of the artwork in comic books is amazing and they are worth quite a bit of money to the right collector.

"Anyway, I didn't call you to discuss my comic book collection, or my lack thereof." Cameron takes a moment and then adds with total earnestness in his voice, "I called to make sure we were still on for this weekend. *And* because I truly was thinking about you . . . I have been ever since Saturday night."

"I have too," I admit quietly. "And yes, we're still on for this weekend."

"Good. I was thinking that I'd make you dinner this time around."

"You're a cook too?"

"I'm not too bad, if I follow the recipe," he says. "So then it's settled. How about you come over to my place on Friday night and I'll make you dinner?"

"Okay, that sounds good. But I feel like I should be doing something too, Cameron."

"You don't have to lift a finger, but if it makes you feel better, you're more than welcome to bring the wine."

When we say our good-byes a moment later, the magnitude of what I agreed to hits me like a ton of bricks. I am going to his house . . . where his bed is . . . just the two of us . . . for several hours. And I have no idea if this falls under the category of second base or a home run, third base or a strikeout, or whatever stupid baseball euphemism Julia uses to describe sex.

Damn that crazy woman. Now she has my head swimming with this garbage and it's not even daylight.

On Thursday night after dinner, Josie asks if she can spend the next night at Carrie's mom's house.

Normally, this wouldn't be a big deal. And the fact that I don't have to get a babysitter for Josie since I have plans on that same night with Cameron is kind of a relief.

One less thing I have to worry about.

But it has the reverse effect on me. Because now in the back of my mind, where it's already overcrowded with baseball stuff for no good reason, I'm going to know that I won't have anyone that I have to come home to. And being the adult that I am, I don't have to come home if I don't want to.

Does that make me irresponsible?

On top of that, it makes me feel incredibly guilty that I'm happy my daughter won't be around to worry about. I feel like the world's worst parent just thinking it. But there it is. It's the truth. Well, maybe the semi-truth.

The more I think about it, the more I resolve that this is the very first time ever since Josie was born that I have even contemplated something even remotely selfish or close to what my life was like before her. So I should be feeling excited and happy, not guilty.

This is what Julia has been telling me the entire time we spoke about it earlier today. Actually, what she really said was this: "Are you effing kidding me?! You're like mother of the year and need to shut the eff up and have sex and like it, dammit!"

I assume she was censoring herself only slightly because her daughter was somewhere in the vicinity when we were talking. So thank God for tiny miracles.

When Friday does come, and after I've dropped Josie off at school, gone to work for a full day, and am sitting on my bed after a long, hot shower wrapped in my robe, contemplating what to wear to Cameron's house in a little while, it dawns on me that I don't have to have sex with him.

I feel like an idiot even worrying about it in those terms. But I think I needed to remind myself that if I do or don't, it doesn't matter. I can take things as slow as I like or as fast as I like. And better yet, I'm pretty sure that Cameron will be okay with whatever I decide.

Not that I wouldn't want to have sex with him after that kiss the other night and the whole sleepwalk sex thing that happened already between us. I'm not a completely clueless person. It's just too much pressure, and what with everything else going on in my life, I shouldn't be adding any more stress and complications right now.

So I'll go for a nice, home cooked meal, have some wine but not too much, and have a sex-free evening with Cameron . . . and then I'll come home to my own bed, alone.

CHAPTER SIXTEEN

The best laid plans . . .

That's what I'm thinking as I plug Cameron's address in to my GPS and drive over to his house. I'm semi-familiar with the area, seeing as how I've lived in Miami all my life, but it never ceases to amaze me all the little nook and cranny neighborhoods in some of the smaller enclaves that I discover the longer I live here.

His modest little bungalow is at the end of a street that is lined with fruit trees, ficus trees, and lots and lots of palm trees. There is a wooden privacy fence with a gate on his property, and it's overgrown with beautiful shrubs and ivy that make it look like it's been there for ages. It makes me think that Cameron's picked the perfect house for himself since it's simple and understated, yet gorgeous and classic . . . much like the man who lives inside of it.

After parking my car in his driveway, I grab the chilled bottle of white wine, get out, and with equal amounts of fear of the unknown and anticipation, I make it up the stone path to his front door and knock.

Cameron opens the door, and immediately I'm in over my head, because he's just so damn handsome and there is no way in the world I'll be able to stop from throwing myself at him. He's wearing beat-up blue jeans with canvas-colored Converse sneakers and an unbuttoned blue and white checkered shirt over a plain white T-shirt that says in dark blue lettering: "Don't trust atoms, they make up everything."

"Hi," he says with a welcoming smile and holds the door wider for me to step inside. "Did you find the place okay?"

"I never knew this road existed, to be honest. But the navigation on my phone got me here in one piece, as you can see." I hand him the chilled bottle of wine, and he thanks me.

"Please, come on in," he says and steps aside to let me pass.

When I cross the threshold and take another step inside, he takes hold of my hand and pulls me closer. Without saying one more word, he presses a light kiss on my lips.

"Hi."

"Hi," I say, a little out of breath from the unexpected kiss so early in the evening's activities. Not that there is a rule that states there can only be kissing after nine p.m., and only if it's a starry night, or whatever stupid rule I'm imagining. Nevertheless, it sets me at ease that it's out of the way, breaking the ice and the mounting tension inside of me. How he knew that I needed that, I don't know. But I'm glad he did it.

Cameron then lets me go and closes the door behind us.

"Dinner is almost done," he says. "I hope you like shrimp."

"I do and it smells delicious."

We're standing in a small foyer that opens up to his living room, which is decorated with a simple, long, dark brown upholstered couch and a big coffee table with matching end tables. The walls are plain white, but the ceiling has the original wood beams from when the house was built, and it's gorgeous.

"Cameron, those beams . . . I love them." I take a step farther into his living room to really inspect the room. "Did you have to restore them or did the house already come with them done like that?"

"Actually, that was the only part that was done. Everything else, from the walls to the hardwood floors, I did myself."

For some reason, this really surprises me. I have him pegged as . . . a nerd. But like the most handsome nerd known to mankind. And definitely not the kind of guy who knows how to restore a house.

I like it.

"Don't look so surprised," he says with a raised eyebrow. "I'm not all about geeky stuff."

He says this as we walk past his mounted television on the wall, which from this angle, I can see has framed artwork all around it that is *Star Wars* inspired.

I laugh hysterically, because really, this is exactly what I pictured and expected from him. "You were saying?"

He turns to look at what has captured my attention, and the poor guy's face goes a little red. Rubbing the back of his neck, he admits, "Yeah, I might have a little thing for *Star Wars* memorabilia."

"They're quite beautiful," I say to him and take a step to inspect them more closely. "Your sister mentioned something about your obsession with all things *Star Wars* that day at the art fair."

They're blueprints of the Death Star, the *Millennium Falcon*, an X-wing fighter, and an AT-AT walker. "You remember that?"

"Of course I do." I remember something else. "Speaking of which, where is . . ."

"*True Love's Kiss?*" he asks, shoving his hands in his jeans pockets. "Follow me," he says.

He leads me out of the living room, which opens up to his kitchen in the back of the house. He walks over to the refrigerator, where he puts the bottle of wine I brought. Looking around his kitchen, I notice that it's not too big and looks to have been updated recently with modern stainless steel appliances. It has a good-sized island with an eating area for two, which I can see he already set up for us.

Past the kitchen, there is a hallway that I assume leads to the other rooms in the house. I panic for a second, thinking no way are we going to his bedroom, but he stops me in the middle of the hall and points to the wall behind me.

I see my sketch that he purchased at the art fair, framed and hanging on the wall by itself. I'm at a loss for words, because other than my own family, I've never been in the house of someone who has bought my work and actually seen it being shown like this.

It makes me a little emotional and proud, because this is *my* hard work on *his* wall, which he deemed worthy enough to present to anyone who may come in here.

"So now that it's just you and me, can you tell what inspired this?" he asks, then leans against the wall next to the framed sketch.

One can barely make out the faint wisps of two faces: a man and a woman. I created all these swirls around them in black charcoal so that if you were looking at it from any angle, you wouldn't be able to identify many, if any, of their facial features. The woman's long hair covers most of their faces, but their lips are connected. Hers are fire engine red, so that it almost looks like a blaze of fire is set in between them from just that one kiss.

I explain all of this to Cameron, who watches me carefully and then tilts his head to look at the drawing again, then I add, "Promise you won't laugh when I tell you what inspired it?"

He nods and says, "Of course."

"You know the story of Sleeping Beauty, right?" He nods again. "I had just watched that recent movie they made about her, and something about that phrase just stuck with me."

"What about it?"

I lean against the opposite wall, staring at the drawing. "True love's kiss . . . it seems pretty inconceivable to me. But the *idea* of it is something else entirely. And whether it could ever happen in real life kept nagging at me. Not to me or anything, just in general. Anyway, the artist in me wanted to believe it, so I started fleshing it out on paper. This is what I came up with. That's it."

"I think that's the most fascinating explanation you could have ever come up with," he says appreciatively. "Seriously, I don't have one creative bone in my body, so I envy those who do."

I've never been one to be able take praise too well; it makes me a bit uncomfortable. So I try to lighten things up by saying, "Well, if you play your cards right, I'll sketch you some *Star Wars* stuff to hang up beside it. Deal?"

Cameron chuckles and puts out his hand for me to shake. "How can I say no to that? Of course you've got a deal."

He leads me back into the kitchen, where I sit and watch him finish preparing dinner. From the looks of it, we're having shrimp scampi over rice and some mixed steamed vegetables. And I'm not lying when I say it smells so good that I can't wait to dig in.

When he's done, he prepares my plate and then his. Then he gets two wineglasses from the cabinet and takes out the bottle of wine. Luckily, I picked white without even knowing it would be a good match for the meal he cooked. So yay for me.

Once he pours our glasses, he picks his up and says, "Here's to playing my cards right," which makes me laugh. "Wait, I'm so sorry, that's not what I meant, Vanessa," he says quickly. "What I mean to say is here's—"

"To playing your cards right," I finish for him with a big grin. "I know how you meant to say it, Cameron. It's okay."

Relief washes over his face as we clink our glasses together, each take a sip, and then dig in.

Cameron can cook. Well. Really, really well.

"This is *sooo* good," I say in between bites of food. "Where did you learn to cook?"

"I told you, if I follow a recipe, there's no way I can screw up." He takes a sip of his wine. "Plus, my parents have in their retirement turned into those foodie type people. You know, the type who are always trying new stuff out at home and at restaurants then posting pictures of whatever they're eating on Instagram. Whenever they come across a good recipe, they'll e-mail it to my sister and me. I don't have a lot of time to cook during the week since I'm either working on lesson plans or grading papers. But on the weekends, I try some of their recipes out . . . the easy ones though."

During the course of the meal, he keeps track of my wineglass, refilling twice without my asking for more. It's a very small thing, but it's appreciated. The smallest of things make the difference. For instance, the way he makes sure to keep his body partially turned and his eyes on me while I'm speaking and shows genuine interest in whatever I'm saying. It tells me that he's attentive, which further adds to his appeal.

"That was perfect, thank you so much."

Cameron clears the plates and I start to get off of my own stool. "No, you sit right there and I'll take care of all of this. That's what dishwashers are for."

While I'm watching him rinse off the plates and set them inside the dishwasher, his back is facing me, and I find myself openly staring and appreciating his physical appearance. He's really, really gorgeous in that not so obvious way, and I wonder if he even knows how appealing that is to a woman. I mean, I've heard through the parent grapevine about that other woman who is after him, but I'm not sure if he would even pick up on it. Or if he would even address it openly with her if he did.

"Hey, Cameron?"

He turns off the faucet and then faces me, wiping his hands with a kitchen towel before flinging it over his shoulder. Then he leans back against the counter and crosses his feet at the ankles, waiting for me to say whatever is on my mind.

"This may be a little personal, but I need to ask you something."

"Go ahead," he says.

"Well, have you ever dated another parent of one of your students before?"

His smile unfurls slowly before he says, "No. Just you."

"And that cake lady? What about her?"

"Who is the cake lady?"

"Well, you see, the parents talk. A lot. It's like this horrible little cesspool of gossip and garbage, really. Kind of like being back in high school, you know?" I take a breath before continuing. "Anyway, they have been saying that there is this one woman who brings you cakes and sweets and stuff to get your attention."

The whole time I'm explaining this information, which yes, is secondhand, he's grinning from ear to ear. Then he pushes off the counter and walks around the island toward me. When he gets to where I'm sitting, he spins my stool around so that I'm facing him. Then he rests his hands just above my knees, his thumbs rubbing my jean clad legs back and forth.

"Vanessa, there is nothing going on between me and this 'cake lady,' and there never will be. I've asked her to stop sending me things, because honestly, it kind of creeps me out. And her baking sucks, by the way."

We both laugh and the tension is diffused as quickly as it appeared.

"The parents talk a lot, don't they?" he asks in amusement.

I nod in agreement. "Yes, they most certainly do, don't they?"

"I bet they're talking about us too." Cameron leans forward, one of his hands coming up to cup my cheek, and asks, "Does that bother you?"

"They or the cake lady?"

"Both," he says with a small laugh.

"Yes and . . . yes."

He leans forward an inch more until there is barely any space between us and I have to open my legs to accommodate him while his mouth trails softly across my jaw and cheek until reaching my ear. He says quietly, "They need to shut up, don't they?"

"Yes," I breathe out and close my eyes.

"I couldn't agree more," he whispers.

Then he places his finger underneath my chin to tilt my face up a little. My hands grip the side of the stool tighter, waiting impatiently for him to finally kiss me. And when he does, it starts out safe and small . . . but as both of our breathing becomes more labored by the slight contact, it quickly spirals out of control.

My hands let go of the stool and reach out to wrap around his waist and pull him closer. His hands rake through my hair and tug gently until my back is leaning against the kitchen island. And our mouths and tongues are seeking more from the other, deeper and deeper, as if we can't get enough of each other.

Rational thought is nonexistent in this moment. It's thrown by the wayside, not to be heard of anytime soon if this keeps up. And the thing is, I'm not sure that I don't want it to keep up. I want him and he wants me, I can tell by every soft growl that escapes him as he continues to explore my mouth and press his body between my legs.

But with that one movement, the responsible and somewhat panicky side of me comes back to the surface, as if to remind me that I cannot be doing this with him so soon. Can I?

Even if the answer is yes, the fact that I'm asking myself that at this juncture scares me enough to pull away and put a stop to this.

"I'm so sorry, Vanessa," he says, his dark eyes softer than I've ever seen them before as he steps back to give me some personal space.

Standing up, and in a sudden urge to get out of there, I say, "It's okay, really. Listen, I have to go. I'm so sorry. Dinner was great, thanks."

Cameron runs his hands through his black locks, clearly confused by what is happening. He tries to stop me by the front door. "Please stay, we'll just talk, I promise."

"I'll talk to you tomorrow, okay?" I stand up on my toes to give him a quick peck on the cheek.

Looking dejected and still confused, he stands as I bolt out the front door and down the walk to my car, where I climb in and go home. Alone.

CHAPTER SEVENTEEN

I make it as far as the end of his street before stopping my car and pulling over.

Taking a deep breath, again and again, helps me to regain focus on the situation, because my head feels as if it was literally spinning for a few minutes.

Skipping from thought to thought, I come to the conclusion that I'm crazy. Well, not crazy, like, loony-bin crazy, but crazy over all of this sex stuff. Poor Cameron, he probably thinks that I'm actually crazy at this point.

I'm an adult, single, red-blooded female who wants to have a sexual relationship with a man that I like a lot and have grown to care about. Has it been in a short time that this has happened? Yes, but the fact remains I'm a grown woman and can do this . . . if I want.

And I do want to do this with him. But now I think I've screwed it all up for good with that scene that just played out a few minutes ago.

God, you're an idiot.

How do I fix this? What could I possibly say to make him understand? I bet he didn't count on this when he signed up to ask me out that first time, and I wouldn't blame him one bit if he didn't want to listen to me attempt to explain myself. Where do I even start?

I make a decision in that instant, which may backfire, but the hell with it. Putting my car back in drive, I spin the wheel and make a U-turn back to Cameron's house. Pulling into his driveway again a second later, I put the car into park and open my door, not letting any hesitation enter into my mind this time. I walk up the steps, but my hand freezes before knocking on his front door for the second time that night.

Then I remember a saying from a book or a movie that goes something like "if you can bear having embarrassing courage for twenty seconds, something good will come of it."

So I knock and the ticking clock of twenty seconds begins as soon as Cameron swings the door open in complete surprise.

"Vanessa, thank God you're back, I was going to call you because I really think we need to—"

"Cameron, can I please come in again?"

He steps aside. "Yes, of course."

I walk straight to his living room while he shuts and locks the front door. When he joins me, I ask him to please take a seat so I can explain myself.

"Vanessa, you don't have to explain yourself. I was pushing you to move too fast and I'm sorry, but when I start to kiss you, my head feels like it's going to explode and—"

Not even recognizing myself, I lean down and grab his face in my hands and kiss him to shut him up. He stills but lets me kiss him fully on the mouth, with just a hint of our tongues grazing each other's. It's enough to dissolve whatever lingering doubts I had earlier and helps to convince me that what I'm about to do is the right thing, right here and right now with him.

I break the kiss and whisper against his lips, "Don't say another word. Okay?"

He nods.

I stand up straight, and with my eyes locked on his, and with the clock running down on the twenty seconds I sorely need to keep my bravery up, I begin to unbutton my blouse. His eyes, already black as the night sky, grow darker with need and want as I reach the final button. When I start to pull the blouse open to slide it off my shoulders, he abruptly stands up and pulls it together again to stop me.

"Why are you—?"

"Are you sure about this?" he asks in a low voice, his hands still holding my blouse together and covering me up.

I search his eyes once more just as the twenty seconds are up and say yes.

"Then I want to be the one to undress you," he says.

I nod in agreement, because I prefer to hand over the reins. He brings my right hand up to hold my blouse together and takes the other in his. He walks me to his bedroom in silence, with the only sound our steps echoing against the hardwood floor the entire way until we reach the foot of his bed. With the small amount of light filtering in from the hallway, I can tell that it's a light-colored comforter thrown over the bed haphazardly, as if he was in a hurry to attempt to make the bed this morning.

He turns me around so that the backs of my knees graze the footboard. I'm in this moment right now with him, and I will follow him down any road he decides to take me on.

I drop my hand, and the unbuttoned blouse separates an inch or two, letting the silk material billow slightly between us as I wait for his next move.

Cameron slowly runs a finger down the sliver of exposed skin, then back up again. It trails up to my collarbone and then down, stopping between my breasts.

"Did you know that attraction is a scientific process that is mostly dictated by our brains, but the body can give off certain telltale signals?"

I swallow some air and let out a breathy no in response. I can see the grin on his face as he dips his head and places a string of kisses across my collarbone. My hands weave into his black hair to bring me closer to him. They stay looped around his neck when he stands up straight again and says, "One physiological response is pupil dilation, it can dictate to a man when a woman is experiencing unbridled lust and vice versa."

Cameron pulls my arms down so that they are hanging limply by my sides. Not a second later, he's tugging the shirt off of each shoulder, and it lands on the floor. My heart is practically pounding in my chest as I note every single action and reaction etched across his face. I feel like putty in his hands, and the more random facts he spouts, the more turned on I become. And if I had to guess, my pupils can't possibly get more dilated right now.

He snakes an arm around my waist and pulls me to him. With our bodies pressed together, he licks his lips quickly before dipping his head once more and kissing me gently; a simple kiss in execution but erotic in its delivery, and it makes my toes curl.

While he's kissing me and his tongue rubs against mine, his hand cups my breast. I moan into his mouth at the sensation when he plucks my nipple between his fingers. Then he pulls away, leaving me heady and desperate for more.

Cameron starts to unbutton my jeans and then slowly unzips them, with his eyes on mine. He crouches down in front of me and starts to slide them down my hips. I kick my shoes off as if they were on fire before he reaches my feet so he can remove them completely.

Now I'm standing before him in only my bra and underwear. For a second, I want to wrap my arms across my chest and cover myself up; my hands twitch with the urge to do just that, but he holds them to the side. From his position, he looks up and says, "Don't, you're beautiful," before placing a kiss on my navel.

When he stands, he starts talking in a low voice again. "A classic symptom of sexual attraction is the release of norepinephrine in the brain. It usually means that your skin will break out in a sweat as a result of the pleasure you're experiencing."

He's saying this as he spins me around so that my back is pressed against his front. And then his hands come around my sides: one sliding up to angle my chin to face him and the other sliding down the length of my torso and farther still, stopping at the edge of my panties.

My breathing is already jagged at best, and if it weren't for his arms around me, I'd probably fall on the floor. The anticipation is killing me, and the science of sex and the calm and erotic way he's explaining it all to me as he touches and kisses me is driving me crazy in the best way possible.

Cameron's hand dips lower still and underneath the small shred of lace fabric. My eyes close and my head falls back onto his shoulder when I feel him touch me there finally, and I moan into the darkness. And with his fingers moving in small circles in just the right spot, he brings me to the brink of climax and then stops as suddenly as he brought me there.

"Here," he whispers and tilts my chin more so his mouth can capture mine.

As our tongues meet again, stroking and stoking the flame inside of me that is dying to burst, his fingers start their ministrations once more, and there is no stopping this time; it's amazing. He swallows my moans, growling into my mouth while he slows the pace of his fingers working against me.

"Are you okay?" he asks tenderly, removing his hand from my panties and swiping a wet trail up my chest.

"Yes."

I'm so okay right now, it's not even funny how okay I am. My chest is heaving as I try to catch my breath when he turns me around to face him again. For the first time, a cocky grin flashes across his face.

"You're sweating," he says with a hint of mischief in his voice.

"I am," I say with an equal amount of mirth. "And you're still dressed."

It's almost as if saying those words out loud sets off a chain reaction inside of me that results in me almost tearing off his button-down shirt and T-shirt. His skin is hot to the touch and smooth with only a smattering of dark hair. And he's fit but not too muscular: as Goldilocks would say, "Just right."

My hands roam the expanse of his chest and down farther still; then he stops me from unbuckling his belt.

"What's wrong? Are we stopping? Please tell me we're not stopping now?" My voice doesn't even sound like my own, but I mean it. I need more from him. I want to feel him move inside of me and finish what we started.

He chuckles lightly and shakes his head once in silent negation. "No, we're not stopping. I just need to get something."

He places me on the bed, and I drag my body up until my head reaches the pillows. Cameron walks around the corner of the bed, his eyes focused on mine while he rummages through his nightstand and takes out a condom.

When he's holding it in between his teeth and going for his belt buckle, I surprise even myself by reaching behind me to undo my bra. It slides down my arms, and I toss it on the floor at his feet. His eyes widen and his nostrils flare as my hands trail down my sides and latch on to the tiny scrap of lace fabric that is my underwear just as he's undoing the buttons of his jeans. And when the buttons hit the hardwood floor with a long ping, I slide my panties down and off my legs, tossing them to land on his discarded jeans.

The urge to cover myself is obliterated. I want him to look at me and appreciate what he sees. In fact, I feel as if my life depends on it suddenly. And his reaction to me being completely bare is worth its weight in gold. Because without another word, he climbs on the bed and pushes my legs apart, staring for a second at the apex of my thighs. It's searing and sensual and makes me want to see every part of him that much sooner.

"Cameron, please," is what I choke out between labored breaths as I writhe on the bed, his dark gaze on me.

On his knees before me, he removes his boxer briefs and tears the condom open finally. I watch as he covers himself with it and leans down over me, holding himself at my entrance. And we both look down between our bodies and watch as he enters me for the first time.

We moan at the feel of it, the sight, one of the most erotic things I've experienced and seen in my entire life. And then he starts to move, setting a pace that makes it beyond pleasurable for me as evidenced by the impending climax that hovers beneath the surface of my already flushed and sweaty skin.

When I do finally break that peak of pleasure, with my legs wrapped around his hips, my hands are gripping his back to guide his movements to a slower pace to prolong the sensation racking my body. Once I reach the crest, he props up on his elbows to look down at me, telling me without voicing it out loud that his desire for me is real and raw. That's when he starts to move faster again, chasing and ultimately reaching his own release. Even with the barrier of the condom, experiencing him pulse inside of me, I feel more like a woman than any other moment before this.

I take his entire weight when he drops his head to kiss and burrow into my neck, my hand caressing his back in slow circles. And the warmth of his body draped over mine is a feeling that I already know I want to experience over and over. As our breathing comes back to normal and I can actually catch a breath and form a coherent string of words, I tap him on the shoulder.

"Am I too heavy?" he asks, propping himself up on his elbows to look down at me.

His hair is a mess from my hands having wreaked havoc in it, and it makes him look even more perfect than before.

I shake my head. "No, you're not too heavy. I was going to ask if you have a T-shirt that says 'I love science,' because as it turns out, I really, really, really love science."

There is a dance that couples do as they sleep that is uncoordinated yet perfectly timed and attuned to their partner's needs and wants as the night goes on.

While this dance happens with Cameron for the very first time—I don't count that other time since I was in a fever fueled haze—I'm amazed at how in sync he is with what *I* want and need from him. Because at one point in the middle of the night, I wake up craving more of him, and he gives himself over to me without question, a sleepy and leisurely discovery of each other's bodies that ends as the morning dawns.

CHAPTER EIGHTEEN

Waking up is hard after getting little to no sleep the previous night.

But waking up is even more difficult when you don't want to leave the bed and the man you're sharing it with.

I had honestly forgotten what it was like, that feeling of being cherished even in sleep by someone you care about. And if last night was any indication, then I'm never leaving this bed. Ever.

Josie.

I practically jump up to sitting position and fling the comforter off of me at the thought of her name. Because I have no idea what time it is, and I'm supposed to be home when Carrie's mom drops her back off after their sleepover.

Cameron, who was sleeping on his stomach next to me, the comforter resting at the dimples on his lower back, and looking absolutely delectable, picks his head up and rubs his face with his hands. "What's going on?" he asks, sounding sleepy and looking over his shoulder to where I'm already gathering up my clothes. "Vanessa, what are you doing?"

"I have to go," I answer as I put my panties on and then spot my bra on the other side of the bed. I rush over to where it is and put it on. "Josie's going to be home in . . ."

Looking everywhere for a damn clock, I finally see one on the nightstand on his side of the bed. "Jesus Christ! She's going to be home in thirty minutes!"

I race through putting on the rest of my clothes, and the whole time I'm aware of Cameron watching me from his bed. He's sitting up by now and leaning against the upholstered tan headboard that we ended up putting to really good use last night.

I rush to the bathroom, run my fingers through my hair, and brush my teeth with my finger. When I look in the mirror, I give my face a once-over and am relieved to see that I don't look like I'm too tired. Or at least not tired enough that anyone would really notice, thank God.

Cameron appears in the reflection, leaning against the doorjamb with just his button-fly jeans on, but the top button is still undone and his arms are crossed over his chest.

"So you're just going to use me for my body and leave?" he asks with a smirk.

Smiling and turning around, I take a couple of steps until I'm standing right in front of him. Getting up on my tiptoes, I give him a kiss. "I'm sorry, but I really do have to get going. If it makes you feel any better, I'd rather I was still in that bed with you."

"I know, and so do I." He reaches up and brushes aside some of my hair, then tucks it behind my ear, his eyes lighting up as they follow the motion. Then he bends down and kisses me again, a light brush of his lips against mine. "Go," he says quietly. "I'll call you later."

The drive home, incredibly, and probably because it's still early in the day, takes me ten minutes. I'm in my house and changing out of my clothes from the night before and taking the world's fastest shower with time to spare. I give myself an air fist bump while running down the stairs, grateful that I didn't screw up this time.

This time?

Wait, is this how it's going to have to be with Cameron? Clandestine nights together so that I can spend the night with him and vice versa? Because that is not at all what I need or even want. Then again, I can't very well have him coming over here whenever I want to do . . . *that* again. And I can't just go over there either whenever I want, because of my responsibilities to Josie. This is probably why I resigned myself to being single all those years ago, because this is already becoming complicated.

Okay, Vanessa, relax. You will figure this out, I say to myself just as the doorbell rings.

I will figure this out, because Cameron does make me very happy and I'm kind of already falling for him. I mean, what's not to fall for; he's almost perfect. I think *almost,* because there is one thing I've learned, a very hard lesson at the time but I know this to be true: no one is perfect.

As soon as Josie is in the house, she takes one look at me and says, "What happened to you?"

This kid and her ever observant eyes never let me get away with a single thing. Not that I'm going to tell her I had sex last night with her teacher or anything specific, but for the life of me, how she's able to always discern when something is up with me boggles my mind.

"I had a late night," I say. "I went on another date with Cameron."

Looking genuinely curious, she asks, "How was it?"

Smiling, I answer, "Really good. I had a great time actually. Thanks for asking."

"Are you going to see him again?"

I nod and say yes, then ask how her evening was with Carrie. She goes on and on about some drama that happened on someone's social media account that they know and how all these random people she also knows from school were commenting on it. Quite honestly, it sounds ridiculous and exhausting. I silently thank God that there was no such thing as social media when I was her age. Whatever happened to good old-fashioned notes? It was one of my favorite pastimes at school.

"See, this is why I don't allow you to have any social media accounts. So you can thank me later if you like, kid."

"Very funny, Mom."

She hooks her book bag on her shoulder, gives me a quick peck on the cheek, and then lets me know she's going up to her room for a while.

Since I haven't had much time to devote to it, and I honestly miss it, I go to the extra bedroom upstairs that I use as my art studio. But first I make a pot of coffee and then fill up a mug with a smile playing on my lips, because I know exactly what I'm going to sketch.

Later that night, after I've devoted a few hours to a couple of new pieces that are somewhat inspired by last night with Cameron, and Josie and I are putting away the dishes from our dinner together, my cell phone buzzes on the kitchen counter.

Josie happens to be closest to it and with a devious smile, swipes it to answer it for me.

Normally I wouldn't care if she did this since it would usually be only family or random work related calls. But it could be my attorney working the petition against Matthew—which she doesn't know about yet, which I really need to take care of sooner than later—and I don't want her to answer it.

In a panic, I grab the phone from her just as she's saying in a very precocious voice, "Hello, Mr. Thomas. How are you on this fine Saturday evening?"

A relief so big washes over me that a potential disaster was averted, but I still want the phone, so I make a grab for it.

She takes a couple of steps backward and out of my reach. "That's good to hear. Oh, and by the way, I finished my science homework already, in case you were wondering."

There is a small pause, and then she says, "That's cool. So you want to talk to my mom or what?"

Another small pause, then before she hands me the phone, she says to him, "Yeah, it was nice talking to you too. Here's my mom for you." She tells me good night and bounces away to her room as if her work was done.

"Hi," I say with a small laugh. "Sorry about that."

"Don't apologize. Josie's a sweet kid and pretty funny. She's actually one of my better students." Then he says, "I've missed you today."

Knowing that he misses me and has no problem with saying it out loud brings a genuine smile to my face, because I've felt the same way. "Me too."

"So what are we going to do about that?" he asks.

And this is when that fear creeps in over how we're going to make this work moving forward. He doesn't have the responsibility of a child, nor has he ever dated someone who has a child, so it frightens me to think that it will be an issue for us.

"Cameron, can I be honest with you?" I ask, and he immediately says yes. "Look, this is going to sound crazy, so bear with me for a second. I *have* missed you today and been thinking about you in general . . . and everything else. What I'm trying to wrap my head around is how we're going to make it so we can see each other like . . . you know, like we did last night. But not every night, because I'm not some nymphomaniac or anything. I'm wondering with me being a single mom and not wanting my daughter to see me acting irresponsibly and making sure I keep things running smoothly, how this is—"

"Vanessa, stop," he says suddenly. "Listen to me for a minute."

"Okay, sorry, I was rambling there, wasn't I?"

With a chuckle, he says, "Just a little bit, but I understand what you're trying to say. I think what we need to do is make sure that we both want to do this. Which I can tell you already, without a doubt, that I really do."

"I do too."

"Good. So next would be stepping into the unknown for the both of us. Because neither of us has ever been in this kind of situation before, so we can figure it out as we go along. But I promise to never put you in a position that would make you feel like an irresponsible parent to your daughter, because that would be the worst thing I could ever do to the both of you . . . I care about you too much to ever let that happen."

"Thank you."

A more perfect answer could not have come out of his mouth if I wrote it for him myself and made him recite it back to me. That is exactly what I needed to hear, and it eases some of the apprehension that has been building up inside of me since this morning.

"Now, getting back to why I was calling. When can I see you again?"

"Soon, and I made good on our deal . . . I have something for you." I smile to myself, thinking of the two new pieces sitting in my art studio, which I hope he likes as much as I enjoyed drawing them.

"My curiosity is piqued. So when can I see this something that you have for me?"

"Obviously it's too late tonight, and I'd invite you over for dinner with us tomorrow, but it's my turn to host the monthly Sunday dinner for my family, so . . ."

"Are you embarrassed by my geeky T-shirts?"

"No!" I say, laughing and thinking of a couple I've seen him wear already. I like them a lot, they kind of go with his whole Professor Indiana Jones meets sexy nerd thing, and plus, they're funny. "Wait, you'd be willing to be thrown to the wolves like that with my family?"

"Well, we just agreed to take things as they come. But that's your call. I would be happy to go but would also be fine if you wanted to take it slower and not have me there."

I chew on my lip. Do I want my family to meet him already?

"I promise I won't wear a nerd T-shirt. I'll look respectable, as if I was a teacher or something."

"Okay, but I'm warning you, my family can be pretty . . . interesting. How about you come over around two o'clock tomorrow then?"

"It's a date." Then he adds, "With a bunch of chaperones present, and I'll be on my best behavior, Scout's honor."

CHAPTER NINETEEN

When I was a kid, my parents had a traditional Sunday dinner, where all of our immediate family would come over and spend most of the day together.

As the years went by, it got to be a little too crazy to keep it going with everyone's schedules. But a few years after Josie was born, my mom wanted to start it up again.

Thankfully, she took my brother's and my advice and made it one Sunday a month instead of weekly. Between working for my dad and spending time with my brother's new little family often, it's not like we don't already spend a lot of time together.

So every month we take turns hosting, and it's my turn.

Usually I start prepping for the meal early in the morning because it is almost like a Thanksgiving spread with all the mouths that have to be fed. I'm an okay cook, but once you start adding on to the volume of food, I get freaked out because I don't want to make so much that my refrigerator is busting at the seams with leftovers. But I also need to make enough that people will be able to eat seconds.

And now I have one more mouth to feed. Yes, it's only one mouth, but that mouth belongs to the man I'm seeing, and this will be the first time he's meeting my family and vice versa. Needless to say, my stress level as I'm starting to chop some of the vegetables and peel the potatoes is at an all-time high, much higher than normal.

Josie assists a little here and there, which really helps me as the time approaches for my family and Cameron to arrive. When the doorbell rings for the first time, she goes to answer it, and I don't even lift my head from the food prep since I already know it's my mom and dad, who always arrive first . . . *and* early, no matter how many times I tell them when to come over on Sunday dinner days.

My parents both come over and say hello to me after gushing over their granddaughter for a few moments. Then the first thing to come out of my mom's mouth is, "Josie says Cameron is coming for dinner too, is that right?"

Immediately followed by my dad saying, "Is that really a good idea, Vanessa? Doesn't it seem too soon for that?"

My mom answers for me, "Oh, stop it! I think it's very sweet that she's including him."

"Allison, I'm only looking out for our daughter and, may I remind you, granddaughter here," he says. My dad's face looks as stern as possible since he usually doesn't win arguments with my mother.

"I'm sure if Vanessa thought it was okay to invite him and Josie is okay with it, then it's okay." My mom then turns to me. "It is okay with Josie, right?"

"Mom, of course it is." I pull off my oven mitts and toss them onto the kitchen counter. "You guys aren't going to give him a hard time, are you?"

My mother points a finger at herself. "Who, me? Sweetheart, who do you think I am? Of course I'm not going to give him a hard time. Your father, however, is another matter entirely."

"This coming from the same woman who asked for his driver's license number already," I say matter-of-factly.

"Providing a driver's license is totally reasonable, Vanessa," my father chimes in.

"That's what I thought too," my mother says.

There is no reasoning with either of my parents at this point, so

I simply puff some air out of my mouth in frustration and finish up the meal. Thankfully, my parents move over to the couch when they see they aren't getting anywhere with me and keep Josie company until the doorbell rings again while my back is turned.

From the commotion at the door, I can tell it's my brother, my sister-and-law, and my niece. I secretly hope that my adorable little niece, Violet, will provide more of a distraction to my parents, and everyone else for that matter, so that Cameron doesn't feel singled out when he does finally get here.

But that is not what happens.

Because not even a minute after I hear the door close behind my brother's family's arrival, the doorbell rings once more.

As luck would have it, my beloved sister-in-law, Julia, opens it. I know this not because I can see it happening . . . but because I can hear her from the kitchen as clear as day, saying to him as she opens the door, "So this is Professor Indiana Jones, huh?"

And right there went my plans for a semi-nice Sunday dinner with my family . . .

"What did I do?" Julia asks a little while later in the kitchen. She's supposed to be helping me get all the food onto serving dishes, but instead she's leaning against the counter with a tall glass of white wine in her hand.

"Do I even need to answer that question?"

She glances over to the living room, where everyone else is seated. Cameron, who I'm convinced is a saint, is sandwiched between my dad and my brother. Whatever they're saying is making him whip his head back and forth between them as if he were in the middle of a tennis match and trying to keep up, but from the looks of it, failing miserably. Meanwhile, my mother is sitting on the other couch, completely oblivious, with Josie and Violet watching something on the television to pass the time until dinner is served.

When Cameron was greeted by Julia, I almost dropped the giant casserole dish I was holding. Thank God that didn't happen. To my surprise, he took the question with a laugh and said hello to everyone, one by one. Then he walked over to me and gave me a bouquet of daisies and a kiss on the cheek.

To say that my heart melted at the earnest gesture and the fact that I could see that he was completely out of his comfort zone already would be an understatement. I thanked him profusely for the flowers, and that's when my brother and dad swooped in and led him to the couch, where he's been stuck for the last ten minutes or so while I've been finishing up.

"You're the one who has the Harrison Ford fetish, not me," Julia says. "Not that that's a bad thing though."

My eyebrows scrunch up in confusion. "What does that mean, exactly?"

She points her wineglass in the general direction of the living room. Then she walks across the kitchen to stand right next to me and whispers, "Just look at him. He's *sooo* hot and dreamy, and I bet . . ."

"You bet what?" I ask.

"I bet he's the kind of guy who totally goes for the gold in bed, if you know what I mean."

Even though I'm slightly horrified by this conversation, I can't help the very distinct and vivid memory that what she is saying brings to the forefront of my mind. Now all I can see in my mind's eye are quick flashes of very erotic images: Cameron sitting up with his back flush against the headboard, his strong hand gripping my hip and the other hand holding my breast to his mouth, sucking the nipple gently between his teeth; I'm moving over him in slow circles and my head's thrown back in complete ecstasy.

"Oh. My. God!" Julia shrieks loudly.

"What happened?" This comes from my mother on the couch, whose head whips around to see what's going on with us.

"Nothing, Mom," I say with a fake smile. "Julia just tasted my meat loaf and thinks it's the best I've ever made."

"Oh good. I can't wait to taste it, sweetheart."

I turn to face Julia and press my finger to my lips. "Would you keep your voice down?"

"You are such a little sneak," she says in a hushed voice with a giant, stupid grin. "You totally did the deed with him, didn't you?"

"Look, if I tell you, will you promise to behave?" I ask her just as quietly. She nods her head like a dog excited to be taken out for a walk. "Okay, the other night we . . . did it."

"Once or twice?"

My eyes go to the back of Cameron's head, still bouncing back and forth between Alex and my dad.

"Vanessa, do not tell me it was more than twice in one night?"

I bite my lip and then shrug my shoulders. "Three times."

Julia doesn't say a word. She simply puts down her wineglass on the nearest surface, then starts to clap slowly.

"Now what is going on in there?" This time it's my brother who is asking.

I grab Julia's hands to stop her stupid golf clap and shout back to him, "Nothing. Dinner's ready, by the way."

As everyone makes their way to the dining room table, I give Julia a stern look. "Listen, I swear to God, you better not say another word or make one of your little comments about it during dinner. This is your one and only warning. Because if you do, I'll be forced to tell everyone else at that dinner table about how you took a dump on the birthing table."

Her mouth drops open in shock. "Alex told you about that?!"

"Yes, so you better watch what you say about Cameron and me sleeping together."

Julia's face goes back to normal, and she calmly picks up her wineglass from the counter as if nothing happened. "I don't have any idea what you're talking about."

"Yeah, I thought so," I say to her back as she's walking away to the dining room.

CHAPTER TWENTY

The rest of dinner went smoothly, but that might have something to do with me being able to keep one nosy sister-in-law in check for the remainder of the evening. Since it is a school night, Josie went to bed about an hour ago, leaving Cameron and me on the couch, alone for the very first time all day.

My feet are in his lap, and he's rubbing them with the right amount of pressure. It feels heavenly, and if he's to keep this up, I may fall asleep right here.

"So your family is something else," he says in the silence between us.

I open my eyes and start to laugh. "That's putting it mildly."

"You're lucky. I don't get to see my family as often as I'd like."

"What about your sister, Natalie? I thought she lived in Miami."

"She was just visiting me that weekend when you met her at the art fair. She lives back in Port St. Lucie," he says, smiling. "I try to make it up that way a couple of times during the summer break, and if not, Thanksgiving, but definitely every Christmas."

"Do you regret coming to Sunday dinner?" I ask jokingly.

It's his turn to laugh now. "Not at all, but . . ."

"But what?" I sit up and pull my feet off his lap. "Did someone say something to you?"

I will kill Julia if she let something slip, but he shakes his head while still laughing.

Then Cameron reaches up and brushes some of my hair off my shoulder. "But I'm hoping you'll show me whatever it is you have for me."

"What I have for you?" My mind goes back and forth so quickly, trying to think of exactly what he's referring to, until it hits me with a bang. "Oh my God! I totally forgot about that."

Jumping off the couch, I stand over him with a big smile on my face, suddenly feeling happy and excited and nervous at the same time. "Come on, follow me."

With his hand in mine, he walks up the stairs behind me into my art studio. "Now you know you must be special," I say to him. "Because I don't let just anyone in here."

"I'm honored," he says while looking around the room. "Vanessa, these are amazing."

I have several pieces that are in various states of completion tacked on the walls and leaning against the wall in small stacks. In the far left corner of the room is my stool, which faces an easel with a blank canvas. My charcoal pencils and oil paints are strewn in organized chaos on the table next to it.

"Why is it blank?" he asks, pointing to the canvas on the easel.

I run my fingers across the slightly ribbed surface and close my eyes. When I open them, Cameron is next to me and waiting for me to explain. "Whenever I leave this room after working in it—even if it's just for a couple of hours or all day and night—I have to leave a blank canvas up on this easel."

He moves to take a seat on the stool behind me. Then his arms wrap around my waist and pull my back to his chest while I explain the reason behind my idiosyncrasy.

"You know how they say life can be like a blank slate, an empty canvas?" I ask him and turn in his arms a bit.

"Yeah."

"It's kind of like that."

"How do you mean?" he asks.

"Well, a blank canvas really isn't blank to me at all." I face the easel. "I look at this and see endless possibilities. I see it becoming something even if it doesn't know what it is just yet. No matter what I do with it, it can always be changed; it can even be painted over to be a blank canvas all over again, so it has a second chance. And sometimes I leave it blank for a bit longer because I need some time to figure out what it wants to be, and a fresh start is the best way to go about accomplishing that. In the end though, it doesn't matter what colors are on it, or if I go outside the lines . . . what matters is the journey it took to get me there."

His finger tilts my chin to look at him again, then he kisses me softly. "You're gorgeous and that was remarkable. Thank you for telling me that." Pressing another kiss on the tip of my nose, then quickly on the lips, he asks, "So what do you see there now?"

"I don't know," I admit with a chuckle. "But yesterday, I saw you."

"Me?"

"Yeah, you." I bring my hand up to cup his jaw and kiss him. Pulling back with a smile, I notice his eyes are still closed. I ask him, "Do you want to see?"

Cameron opens his eyes and excitedly says yes. So I extract myself from his arms and pick up one of my many portfolios. This one in particular has mostly charcoal drawings. Thumbing past other works, I find the two I'm looking for.

"I really hope you like them," I say and then ask him to close his eyes. "No peeking until I say so."

I tack them up on the opposite wall, and without further ado, I tell him to open his eyes and see for himself.

"Are you kidding me right now?" he asks with a huge grin on his face. "Seriously, this is a joke, right?"

I shake my head. "No, I did these yesterday. They're for you, only if you want them, of course. I mean, art truly is subjective, so I get it if you don't want them, and I wouldn't be offended or anything."

"They're awesome!" He stands up and takes the few steps over to where I am so he can look closer. His eyes roam over the first one and then the second. Then, as if something caught his attention, he goes back to staring at the first one. "Wait a second. Is that me?"

"Yes."

The drawing in question is of Darth Vader, but his mask is cracked and has fallen off half his face. Instead of sketching the face of the actor who played him in the movie, I drew half of Cameron's face. I don't know why I ended up doing it like that; maybe because I know how much of a fan he is of the movies, or maybe because I was just on a high from having spent the night with him for the first time. Either way, I thought it looked pretty cool.

The other is a sketch of Han Solo frozen in carbonite. That one I drew from memory, and also maybe because Harrison Ford reminds me a lot of Cameron.

"Vanessa, these are . . . this is . . . I am so blown away right now, I don't even know what to say."

"So you like them?" I ask him with a modest smile.

"I love them, and if they're really mine, I'm immediately getting them professionally framed." He stops and looks back at the draw- ings and then back to me, but with a sneaky smile on his face. "But only after you do one more thing."

Cameron walks over to the table where I keep all my charcoal pencils and randomly picks one up. He comes back and hands it to me. "I want you to sign them for me."

I do as he asks, and when I'm done, he grabs my face in his hands and brings his mouth over mine. With each brush of his lips and stroke of his tongue, I feel more breathless and utterly lost in him. In the back of my mind, I think that maybe true love's kiss isn't just something to read about or see in the movies. I *want* to believe in the fairy tale, as it turns out. And with the way he holds me so reverently, and the faintest skim of his fingers trailing down my neck, tracing the bared skin of my shoulders, then down the length of my arms until he captures my fingers in his, I find myself able to believe in it a little bit more.

When Cameron pulls away, he keeps our fingers entwined. "Thank you so much. I have no way of expressing how much it means to me that you drew those just for me."

"You're welcome," I whisper, still a little breathless from that last kiss.

He searches my face for a second, as if trying to commit every single wrinkle, freckle, and beauty mark to memory. "It's getting late."

I'd be a liar if I didn't feel a pang of disappointment that he has to go home, but this is what the whole dating a single parent comes with. Even though he seems to be okay with it all now and has told me as much, my fear is that it will get to be a hassle for him not having the freedom to do certain things whenever he, or I for that matter, wants. But I remind myself that we did agree to move forward and to take things one step at a time. So I'm willing to let go of the disappointment for now and try not to dwell on it.

"Yeah, it's a school night," I say with a small smile. "You have to wake up early and mold the minds of young children."

He chuckles at that, then lets me go so I can untack the drawings from the wall. After I've put them in an old portfolio I have lying around, I hand it over to him.

When we reach the front door, he pulls me to him again, wrapping his arms around me in a big hug.

"I want to see you again, Vanessa. Soon."

I smile into his chest before pulling back to look at him. "Me too. Soon."

He laughs. "Would you be open to the idea of letting me take you and Josie out to dinner this week?"

"I think it's very sweet of you to include her, and yes, I think that would be great," I say and mean it, because it shows how seriously he is taking this and trying to make this work between us.

Then Cameron kisses me one more time before leaving for the night.

With my lips aching in bliss from his kiss and my heart thumping away with happiness and excitement, I watch him until his taillights are a distant memory in the darkness.

CHAPTER TWENTY-ONE

Sometimes I think to myself, *What if?*

What if I never went away to college and met Matthew?

What if I had an abortion like he wanted me to, or what if I gave the baby away for adoption to a couple who couldn't have children of their own?

What if I had decided to run away to Paris to live the life I had dreamed for myself ever since I was a little girl, before Matthew?

The answer is simple: Josie.

Because if I had never gone to college and met Matthew, if I had decided to run away to Paris to live out my dream, if I had had an abortion or given the baby up for adoption . . . there would be no Josie. I have a hard time picturing what my life would be like without her in it. She completes me in a way that I could never have imagined before her.

She is the one great thing I've accomplished in my life and was meant to do, and I'll be damned if anyone or anything will ever hurt her in any way, shape, or form.

But . . . what if *I* am the person who hurts her? I never took into account that I could ever be the source of so much of her pain. I always believed that our bond was too strong to ever be shaken. I am finding out the hard way that the best of intentions are not necessarily the best way to handle things. That keeping things hidden from the ones you love most is almost a guarantee that the bond will shatter from the weight of those secrets.

And as with most things in life that damage your very fragile existence, you never see them coming.

―――――◆―――――

A few days later, I take Cameron up on his offer to take Josie and me out to dinner. It has to be a little earlier than usual since it is another school night though. So I made plans to have him pick us up a little after five o'clock, which Josie thinks is hilarious since that's just about making it early-bird senior-citizen dining hours, according to her.

I'm in my bedroom freshening up from the long workday when I hear the doorbell ring, signaling Cameron's arrival. Josie's muffled feet running across the living room lets me know that she's letting him in, so I don't have to go downstairs just yet. As silly and immature as it seems, the thought that I'm going to be seeing him again in a couple of minutes excites me; my stomach swirls and does mini somersaults as a result. I swear that if someone told me I'd be experiencing that feeling again in my lifetime, I would have called them a liar. Stranger still is the fact that I can admit to myself that I missed it to begin with, that I had been secretly wanting to experience the pull of attraction and strong feelings for someone else all these years.

It may seem crazy given the short time we've been together, but the feelings I have for Cameron have gone beyond like and well into possibly love. I wouldn't dare say it aloud to anyone—not even to myself—but I know that every part of me is aching for him, and not just in the physical sense.

"Mom, are you almost ready?" Josie yells up the stairs.

Checking myself in the mirror one more time before heading downstairs, I shout back, "I'll be right there!"

Cameron is waiting for me at the foot of the steps. He runs a hand nervously through his jet-black hair as he takes me in from my head to my toes, making me worry that there's something wrong.

Walking right up to him, I ask him quietly, "Is everything okay?"

"Yes, more than okay," he says. "It's just . . . it's just that you're so beautiful and amazing that every time I see you I wonder what a woman like you could ever be doing with a man like me."

I loop my arms around his neck, bringing my face a breath away from his. "I ask myself the same exact question all the time . . . but the other way around."

The corners of Cameron's mouth curl up in a smile when I close the almost miniscule distance between our lips and press a kiss there.

"Ahem." That comes from Josie, who is still in the room. For a moment, I'm mortified, but she quickly adds, "It's okay, Mom, I was only joking. You guys are pretty cute together, even if Mr. Thomas is my science teacher."

She's got a huge grin on her face when I look at her over Cameron's shoulder. When I notice that she's right by my purse, which is sitting on the kitchen counter, I ask her to grab it for me so we can start heading out.

Leaning over the counter, Josie yanks the corner of my purse, and I watch as it slowly starts to tip and then falls completely over to the side as the contents spill out all over the kitchen floor.

"Sorry, Mom," she says and gets on her knees with my now empty purse in her hand. "I'll put everything back together for you."

Cameron draws me closer and links my hands in his. "I know it's only been a few days since . . ." He hesitates a second, searching my eyes. "But it's different, right? You feel it too."

The undercurrent of emotion is evident in his eyes and by the way his fingers grip mine lightly. I know that whatever it is between us is clear as day to both of us, and I don't want to lose whatever it is. But I also don't want to jinx myself either. That's why he didn't have to ask me if I feel it too, since I know exactly what he means.

"It's good different, Cameron," I say to him. "Really good different."

"So you're not scared off by it?"

"A little," I admit with a small smile. "But it's only because I've been alone for so long that it takes some getting used to."

"I never thought I'd say this to someone so soon, but I think I'm—"

"Mom!" Josie yells.

I look over to the kitchen counter, where she's standing again. "What's the matter?"

"When were you going to tell me about this?!"

In her left hand she's holding a piece of paper. Having no idea what it is and wanting to defuse an already awkward situation with Cameron present, I ask her calmly, "Josie, sweetie, what are you talking about?" I turn to Cameron and excuse myself. And then I realize what she's holding: Matthew's letter.

My heart sinks as tears well up in Josie's eyes.

"Sweetie, I was going to tell you, I swear." My voice quavers slightly.

"When? In between your dates with him?" Her voice drips with venom and raw anger as she points behind me to where Cameron is probably wondering what is going on. "When, Mom?"

Cameron looks extremely uncomfortable at what is playing out in front of him. He rubs the back of his neck with his hand and starts to say something, but I stop him. "Cameron, I'm so sorry, but can we reschedule for another night?"

"Sure, sure," he says with a polite smile. "I'll let myself out and I'll call you later to make sure everything is okay."

"Okay, thanks." He leaves and I turn back around to Josie, who is still seething with anger.

She has every right to be upset. I have completely let her down. But how do I explain that it was only to protect her? That I thought it wasn't the right time to tell her about what Matthew has been trying to do. She knows about him in the sense that she knows I didn't have a miracle pregnancy, but she doesn't know all the details of what happened then and obviously nothing of what's happening now. Where do I even start?

"Listen, sweetie, let me explain."

She waves the letter in the air. "I read in the letter that my dad wants to meet me! He sent it months ago! When were you planning to fit it in?!"

"Josie, I—"

"Forget it, I don't want to hear it! It's too late, Mom!"

She storms off, making a beeline to the stairs.

"Josie, wait, I need to talk to you about this!"

Turning around at the foot of the stairs, she wipes her eyes, then sounds and appears eerily calm when she says what she says next.

"I don't ever want to talk to you again. Stay away from me."

She continues up to her room, slamming the door behind her and leaving me wondering what I can possibly do or say to fix this.

CHAPTER TWENTY-TWO

I knew that I would have to tell her eventually, but something inside of me kept saying it was never the right time. Or maybe, just maybe, I was hanging on to the hope that I wouldn't have to ever tell her. It sounds awful to admit that, but I can't lie to myself anymore. I took the easy way out—the coward's way out—by not saying a word about it to her.

It's a fine line to walk as a parent: steering your children to believe that everything is great when it's anything but. And when they do find out . . . the pain they inevitably experience as a result of your negligence is something that you wish you could take away from them.

I've been sitting here for the past half hour alone, trying to come up with a way to start this talk with Josie, but also giving her time to process the letter from Matthew. But I can't put it off anymore . . . it's time to tell her everything.

My legs trudge up the stairs as if I have weights strapped to my ankles. I approach her door and knock hesitantly.

She shouts, "Go away!"

"I can't do that, Josie," I say and open the door.

Josie is curled up in her bed. Her back is facing me and the slight shake of her shoulders lets me know that she's crying. My heart breaks into a million pieces at the sight of her like this. But I'm here to make this right and try not to cry too much in the process.

"Mom, I told you to go away," she says in a small voice, sounding more like the Josie I know . . . in between sniffles.

I sit down on her bed. "And I told you I couldn't do that right now. I need to talk to you about your father."

"It doesn't matter anymore, I—"

"Just listen to me, and then I'll leave you alone, I promise, okay?"

Josie doesn't say anything to this, so I take a shaky breath, hoping that after I'm done, she'll have a better perspective on my past with her father and how it's shaped the decisions I've made for us.

"Your father and I were so in love, once upon a time. We were together for a very long time, since college, which is where we met." I laugh at the memory, still fresh in my mind. "Did I ever tell the story of how we met?"

Josie doesn't turn around, but I can see her head shake against the pillow she's resting on.

"Well, I was running around campus trying to find my next class—it was the first day of my junior year—and I was having the worst day. Just everything that could go wrong went wrong. So when I finally got to the right building, I was in a full-on sprint, and when I turned the corner I ran straight into your dad.

"I was such a little pain in the ass that I actually yelled at him for getting in my way. Well, he thought that was the funniest thing ever. Because he let me yell and yell at him while he picked up all my books from the floor and then at the very end when I was walking away to class—he was so smooth about it and smiling—he asked me, 'What's your name and when can I run into you again?'"

"That's not very funny," Josie says and rolls over onto her other side, finally, to face me. "Or smooth, Mom."

I take the opportunity to lie down on my side facing her to continue the story.

"To me, it was. Plus—this was the best part—he was waiting for me outside of the class as soon as I got out."

Her face lights up at that, so I go on again, knowing I'm going to have to hit the hard part sooner than later.

"So, we started dating . . . and then fell in love, of course. We were so different though, now that I think back on it."

"How do you mean?" she asks.

"For one, I was an art major. Your dad was a finance major. That right there was enough. He was always a realist, when I was always the dreamer. But they say that opposites attract, and for us it worked. By the time we were seniors, we had our own apartment together off campus, and it was so great. Even after graduation, with him starting to work at his father's financial firm and me getting my feet wet in the local art community, it was all like a dream come true, and it was like this for a couple years. Then . . ."

"Then I came along to ruin everything," she says.

"Oh no, sweetie." I reach up and brush aside some of her hair from her forehead. "Don't ever say that. You didn't ruin anything."

"So then what happened?" she asks with genuine curiosity.

"I realized that I was pregnant with you, and I'm not going to lie to you and say that I was happy at first. Honestly, I was terrified. I was young and had my future already planned out in my head, just waiting for me to start living it. But the more I thought about it, the more I fell in love with you, and I hadn't even met you yet."

Josie wipes a tear away from her eye and says, "You're just saying that to make me feel better."

Taking her hand in mine, I shake my head. "No, I'm not just saying that. I mean it with all my heart, Josie. You were like this little unknown thing inside of me that was made with so much love—"

Her face scrunches up. "Mom, that's gross."

We both laugh, more of the tension that had been suffocating us easing its way out of the room.

"It's the truth though. Yes, you were making me puke my guts out at the drop of a hat and making me want to sleep for most of the day *and* night, but it was more than that. It's hard to put into words what being pregnant is like. It's like trying to explain a sunset to someone who has never seen one before. Or trying to explain what falling in love is like for the first time if they haven't felt their heart literally ache with that same feeling for someone. You're just going to have to trust me on this one."

"My dad though, he didn't feel the same way, did he?"

"I—"

"Mom, I want you to tell me the truth."

"I am, sweetie. It hurts still when I think about it, and I haven't spoken about it to anyone in years, so you'll have to forgive me if it takes me a while to get it all out, okay?"

She nods and grips my hand a little tighter.

"At first he seemed okay with the idea of having a baby. I mean, we had been together so long that of course we had spoken about marriage and all that good stuff. But I think the idea of kids was in the distant future for him. Definitely not something that he was prepared to handle that soon out of college and while trying to get his career off the ground.

"So he left . . . and I was devastated. But I had to keep going for you."

Josie moves over, closer to me, and then rolls over so that I'm spooning her. "I'm sorry he did that to you, Mom."

"I'm sorry too," I say.

After a long moment of both of us being completely silent and still, she asks quietly, "So then what happened?"

"You happened. Actually, you happened earlier than expected is what happened. I went into labor with you about two weeks early, and oh my God, talk about being terrified? I was scared to death. But your Uncle Alex was there for me the whole way . . . and you."

"What do you mean?"

"He was there in the room when you were born," I say with a laugh and pull her tighter and closer against my chest. "But somebody decided to take their sweet time in making their world debut. When you finally did come, the nurse took you away to clean you up, and that made me even more scared because you weren't crying." I place a kiss on the top of her head as I remember that awful feeling. "Because they tell you in birthing class that babies generally cry when they're born. Not you though. You came out quiet as a little church mouse. Then the nurse brought you over to me all swaddled up in this pink blanket—I still have it somewhere in the house, by the way—and they put you in my arms. I looked at your beautiful, perfect, tiny face and I was in love; head over heels in love with you."

Josie pulls away and then rolls over again to face me. "And my dad?" she asks softly.

"No, sweetie, he wasn't there. He hasn't known anything about you and me since the day he left the both of us." Pausing to let that settle for a second, I reach out and grab her hand, linking our fingers together. "But you look like him."

Her eyes light up a little. "How?"

"Well, the eyes, for one, they're definitely your dad's eyes." I tap her nose with a finger. "And this nose is definitely your dad's nose. And every so often, you'll make a certain face, and I swear it feels as if I'm talking to your father all over again."

We're both smiling now and are much less stressed than before I walked into this room. But now I have to explain about the letter and what's going on with it and why I've kept it from her. So I gather up my last bit of courage.

"Josie, about the letter you found . . . I'm sorry, I'm so very sorry about not telling you about it sooner. I wanted to, I really did, but I kept chickening out."

"Why?"

"I just got freaked out by it, I guess. I hadn't heard from your dad in years, and then he sends that letter and I . . . I think there was a part of me that didn't want to have to face him ever again after what he did to us. But the more I think about it, it's really that I didn't want him to ever hurt *you* again. Me, I'm a big girl and I can take it, but you . . . I can't let him break your heart twice."

She looks up at me, her big blue eyes shining with the residue of unshed tears. "Mom, I'm a big girl now too."

"You are." I take a deep breath and say what I came here to really say to her all along. "So if you want to meet him, just say the word, and I'll call him."

Josie chews on her bottom lip for a few seconds, then finally says, "Yes, I want to meet him. I've always wondered about him, and after reading that letter, I just kind of want to see him for myself, you know?"

I nod in understanding, because I do, I get it. If I were in her shoes, I'd be more than curious at this point to put a face to the ghost that has been in our lives all this time. "I get it, kid. And I'll call him myself to set it up, okay?"

"Will you be okay though, Mom? What's going to happen now with you?"

"What do you mean?" I ask her. "With your dad, I'll be fine, if that's what you're worried about. I'll put on my big girl panties and deal with it like the grown-up that I am."

We both laugh again and then she says, "No, I mean with Mr. Thomas. I'm sorry I said those things in front of him. It was kind of embarrassing."

"Oh, don't worry about that. I'll call him later and work it out."

"He doesn't know about any of this, does he?"

I shake my head and think to myself that I'm going to have to figure out how to go about telling Cameron about what is going on with me and Josie's father.

"Are you . . . never mind."

"What?" I ask, smiling.

"Well, I was wondering if how you explained being in love with my dad, if you've ever felt that way before or since . . . or like with Mr. Thomas."

"I don't know if I'm in love with Cameron, or Mr. Thomas, if that makes you more comfortable," I say and she giggles. "But I do know that when I am with him, he makes me feel something that I haven't felt in a very long time."

"That's good, right?" she asks.

"Sweetie, it's very good, but also very scary. But don't worry about that right now. Let's just get through this and then I'll figure out what's going to happen with Cameron, okay?"

"Okay."

"Is there anything else you want to ask me? Because now's the time."

She genuinely looks as if she's thinking very hard through every little thing that she could possibly need answers to and then shakes her head. "No, I'm good."

Dropping another kiss on her forehead, I pull away and sit up again. "So I have to go and make some calls. If you need anything, just let me know."

As I approach her door to leave, my back facing her, she says, "I love you, Mom, and thanks for not chickening out on me thirteen years ago."

"I love you too, and you're welcome, kid."

And when I leave her alone finally and close her door behind me to walk back downstairs, I think to myself that it was the best decision I ever made.

CHAPTER TWENTY-THREE

The next day feels like a freaking tornado landed on my head in the form of phone calls with my attorney that go back and forth for most of the morning until finally a date is set for Josie to formally meet Matthew: this Saturday.

It's only a couple of days away, but I'm already extremely anxious, since it will be the first time I'll be seeing Matthew in thirteen years. And it's not because I have feelings for him. It's more that I have no idea what to say to him that doesn't involve me cursing him out for leaving us high and dry from one day to the next. So I'm working on this little by little as the day approaches. Because the last thing I want to do is look anything but civil and well-adjusted in front of my daughter when this meeting happens. I need to be able to show her that I can handle it, for her sake as well as my own.

The next order of business is letting my family know. This normally wouldn't be a big deal; or maybe it would, I don't know. But considering how close my family is, and with them knowing how much of a mess I was after Matthew left us . . . well, I'm worried they may think I'm crazy for allowing it, especially Alex, who has been the father figure to Josie all these years that Matthew has been MIA.

So it's with great trepidation that I make a few more calls before leaving the office and ask everyone if we can gather at Alex's house for an impromptu family meeting. Luckily, they all agree. And thankfully, nobody asks too many questions.

That is, until my dad shouts from his office as I'm getting ready to head out and pick up Josie at school. "What's this about a meeting at Alex's? Why can't you just tell me what's going on when I'm right here, Vanessa? And this better not be anything about running off with that Cameron fellow."

"I'll see you at Alex's house. I want to tell all of you at the same time. And no, this is not about me running off with that Cameron fellow," I answer him matter-of-factly and in order of questioning, then leave the office.

Cameron . . . dammit, I forgot to call him back last night.

He called just as he promised he would to check up on me after the disaster that was supposed to be our first attempt at going out with Josie. But I was so worn out emotionally from dealing with the fallout of my screwup that I didn't answer. And if I'm being honest with myself, I also didn't know how to go about tackling this issue in my life with him.

I mean, it's one thing to be a single parent, but it's quite another when you throw in the missing link of the dad to the mix after so many years. Maybe this wouldn't be a big deal to most single parents who date. But for me, this is a brand-new ball game, and I don't even know where to start explaining it to Cameron. The thing is that I *want* to be able to tell him and not keep secrets from him. I don't want to have this big thing sitting between us and holding us back in any way. Especially if I truly feel the way I think I'm feeling about him and vice versa.

I also am feeling a tremendous amount of guilt over worrying about this thing with Cameron, because I don't think I should be thinking about him right now. And I feel more guilty that I'm even considering seeing him or spending time with him when my daughter so obviously needs me. So I'm trying to figure out how to balance what my daughter needs with what I can give Cameron. Which isn't really easy to do when you're me and haven't been in a relationship in so long to begin with.

I'll figure it out, I hope.

After picking up Josie, I arrive at Alex's house a short while later to find my parents already there, waiting for me. The one time I wish they could have picked to be late would be today. But no, they of course have to beat me here, even for my own family meeting.

When I walk in the door—having let myself in with the spare key—my family is all assembled in the kitchen, whispering among themselves. My brother sees me first and makes his way over to me, concern clouding his features.

"What are you doing, Vanessa?" he asks in an even lower voice.

"Josie," I say to my daughter, who is already making her way to Violet. "Please let me talk to your uncle for a minute, sweetie. I'll be right there."

"Sure, Mom."

Alex grabs my upper arm and pulls me into the living room. "What in the hell is going on?"

I tell him everything that happened the night before, from Josie finding the letter up to this morning, when I was able to agree to a date and time for Josie to meet her father. To his credit, Alex doesn't say a word. He lets me explain and takes it all in. As always with him, he'll analyze the situation really quickly but very methodically, taking everything under consideration before commenting. It's probably why I always run to him first whenever I have a problem. That and I can trust him with everything and anything in my life, including Josie's best interests. And if he's reading this situation as well as I think he is, then he knows this is the best way to approach it.

"Can I be there when he meets Josie on Saturday?" he asks.

Smiling, I hug my baby brother, who has always been the more responsible one out of the two of us. "No, I have to do this by myself, Alex. But thank you for asking."

"Are you sure?" he asks, this time with a little trepidation in his voice. "I won't say anything, you have my word."

Pulling back, I see that he's worried about something. "What's wrong?"

"I'm like her dad, Vanessa. I don't want to lose that."

"I promise you, that will never happen." I reach up and kiss my brother on his cheek. "You have *my* word."

Then he smiles that dimpled smile of his that lets me know that everything is going to be okay and that he thinks I'm doing the right thing. Well, he also tells me all of this as I'm walking with him to drop this bomb on my parents' laps, who don't know a thing about what's been going on. And the funny thing is, I totally believe him.

"That went pretty well, don't you think?" I ask Josie on the drive back home. "Your grandparents are still in shock, but that's to be expected."

"Mom, I'm pretty sure they think you've lost it," Josie says.

"Yeah, I think you're right, kid."

My parents were beside themselves. I can't say that I blame them either. But thankfully, they were able to contain their thoughts and not say too much in front of Josie. Once they could see that she genuinely wanted to move forward with this, they bit their tongues.

It also helped that Alex was in my corner and expressed his encouragement, which was great for Josie to see, because it gave her a boost of confidence after seeing my parents' initial reaction. Because in the end, this is her decision. For her to know that we will all stand behind her is the most important thing.

After we get home and run through the usual routine of home-work and dinner, Josie calls it a night. I kiss her on the forehead and tell her I love her before she's off to bed. This leaves me with one thought, or rather, person running through my mind that I need to address: Cameron.

I call him, and he answers on the second ring. "Hi, I was hop-ing I'd hear from you. Is everything okay?"

"I'm fine and it's a really long story."

"Does that mean you're not going to tell me or that you want to tell me?" he asks. "Because if it's too personal, I completely understand."

For a second, I'm actually considering not telling him. That I should break it off here with him before it goes any further so I don't have to explain and don't have to worry about what he'll think of me. I also feel that guilt creeping in again that I shouldn't be worry-ing about this part of my life when I'm needed elsewhere. But in a flash it's gone when I hear his voice, calm and soothing, asking me if I'm sure everything's okay with Josie and me.

And for now, that's enough, so I tell him everything.

He lets me talk and only asks a few questions here and there. And I thank God for that, because it makes it that much easier. Which I don't know if I deserve, really, after having essentially kept him in the dark, thinking there was absolutely no drama in my life, when in fact, it was the polar opposite.

"Can I ask you something?"

"Sure, anything."

"Were you ever going to tell me?"

I puff out a breath and answer truthfully, "I don't know. But to be fair, I don't know if I wanted to tell anyone. It's embarrassing in a way."

"How so?"

"He left me. Sorry, I mean, he left us. I'm over it, but sometimes I can't help but wonder if it's something I did or said, or if it was—"

"Vanessa," he says suddenly. "We haven't been seeing each other that long, which we sorely need to address soon, I hope, by the way." He clears his throat nervously and then says, "But I can tell that you are an amazing woman and an even more amazing mother. So if I had to guess, it was him and not you or Josie that had anything to do with his decision."

I didn't know I needed someone other than my family to tell me this, but I did. And I genuinely feel a little lighter with Cameron seeming to be good with this new development.

"Okay, enough about me. How are you? And I know I've said it before, but I truly am sorry about last night."

"I know," he says, then goes very quiet. I've pulled the phone away from my ear to make sure he's still on the call when he speaks up again. "I did mean it when I said that I really would like to see you again, but I'm kind of afraid to ask with everything that is going on in your life."

"I want to see you again too," I admit. And before I can talk myself out of it, I ask, "When?"

"Now."

Laughing at his eagerness and honesty, I wish I can say yes, but it's just not that easy for me. "I can't right now. But maybe tomorrow night?"

"I'd like that."

"Okay, let me get off the phone and see if I can get a sitter, and I'll text you with the details."

"Sounds good," he says. "And Vanessa?"

"Yes?"

"Thank you for telling me. And I'm sure everything is going to work out for the best. You'll see."

We end the call, I make plans for Josie to go to Alex and Julia's house after school tomorrow, and I . . . well, I hope that Cameron is right and that everything will work out for the best.

CHAPTER TWENTY-FOUR

Preoccupied is the best way to describe how I am when I meet up with Cameron at a small café by my house. I mean, it's not because of him being boring or monotonous. If anything, he's charming and witty, and adorably handsome as usual.

It's me.

I can't stop worrying about Josie, or worrying about this meeting with her dad in a couple of days, or worrying how I'm going to feel when I see Matthew for the first time in years . . . and definitely thinking of how I'm going to take hearing him talk about his new life.

I didn't realize that would bother me so much, because of course, he had to go and get himself a new life at some point. The only problem is that I never did; my whole life has consisted of being a single parent. Only recently did I allow myself to venture out and see what's available for me . . . and that's when I found Cameron. Which is great, it really is. But I can't help the nagging feeling that I should be home, acting more like that same parent who gave up everything to be there for her daughter.

"Vanessa?"

Cameron's concerned voice snaps me off of the runaway train that is barreling through my brain. He reaches across the table and takes my hand in his, and I apologize for not paying attention . . . again.

"It's okay, you seemed like you were somewhere else there for a minute. Is everything all right? Is there anything I could do to help?"

"I'm fine, or I will be fine once this weekend is over," I say and notice the worried crease in his forehead. "I'm so sorry, and I keep saying that, I know, but I can't help it right now. My brain feels like it's in overdrive."

He nervously looks around before leaning across the table and kissing me. It's a quick press of his lips against mine, but it's enough to bring me back to the here and now and focus on him. "Why did you do that?"

"I don't know," he says, looking unsure still and running a hand through his hair. "No, that's not true. You looked as if you needed it and I . . . I really wanted to."

Grinning, I lean forward and take his face in my hands, pulling him toward me, and kiss him this time, trying to help ease his mind and at the same time keep me grounded to this moment with him.

When I pull away, he brings his hand up to cup my face and rubs his thumb gingerly across the apple of my cheek. "Why did you do that?"

"I needed it and . . . I really wanted to."

Sitting back down, he drops his hand and curiously tilts his head to the side. "Can I ask you something?"

"Sure."

"Do you regret doing what we did the other night?"

I shake my head instantly. "No, why do you ask?"

"I just wanted to make sure that you still felt the same."

I thought I'd made it clear that I had wanted to let that happen with him. I mean, I was the one who turned around and took the leap of faith. Do I feel conflicted about being here with him now? That's a whole other issue in and of itself that I don't want to tackle right now.

Seeing the look on my face, he says, "I'm sorry. I shouldn't be making you worry about anything when you have so much going on already."

"Cameron, yes, things are crazy right now, but they should settle down. And, not for nothing, but this is all kind of new to me in a weird, late bloomer kind of way."

Leaning back in his chair, he chuckles at that. "You are definitely not a late bloomer, Vanessa."

"Well, what else would you call it?"

He crosses his arms, covering up his clever and cute black T-shirt that has an image of Darth Vader on it that says "Come to the nerd side, we have Pi."

"Hmm, let's see." Then he brings his finger up to push his eyeglasses up the bridge of his nose and says in a sure voice, "You're methodical and confident, even though you think you aren't half the time. You're beautiful and smart, and probably the most creative person I've ever met. And all of that is sitting right in front of me, which I still can't wrap my head around."

I blush at his compliments and say, "How did you get to be such a nice guy?"

"Don't use that word, 'nice.' It's the kiss of death."

Laughing now, I say, "No, it's not. At least not for me it isn't."

"Haven't you ever heard the saying 'nice guys finish last'?" he asks. "That's me in a nutshell."

"I don't believe that," I say. Leaning forward again, I rest my elbows on the table and prop my chin in my hands. "I love that you're so nice and patient with me and willing to put up with all this craziness in my life."

And I really do believe that, because a lot of men would have run in the opposite direction after the other night. But he's been so understanding and encouraging, which makes me feel terrible for not being able to do much more than this right here with him, right now. The logical and responsible part of my brain wishes I could tell him that this, us, is bad timing and maybe we can put it on the back burner for a little while as things move along with Josie and Matthew. But then the emotional side of my brain doesn't want to let him go. The thought of losing him would hurt, I know it. Because I do have feelings for him, just as I know he has feelings for me . . . but I don't know if I'm ready to say it or to hear it or even admit it out loud to myself. So I think the way to go is to keep him, but at arm's length for now, or at least until the dust settles with everything else.

After I notice the time and tell him I have to go and pick up Josie, he walks me to my car. I can't help but notice the uncertainty in his eyes in the way he sneaks a glance at me every so often as we're approaching my car. I want to be able to say all the things that are in my heart and on the tip of my tongue to alleviate his concerns, and mine, for that matter, but I can't right now. Seeing him trying to piece together what is going on in my head and heart makes me want to comfort him, which honestly scares me to death.

"So, I'll see you again soon?" he asks, slightly unsure.

"Yes, you will. I promise."

He moves toward me and takes my face in his hands, searching my face and my eyes for something . . . some telltale sign that will defuse this unknown between us. "I need you to know that I want more from you."

"Cameron, I—"

"Wait, let me finish." He kisses my cheek and then the corner of my mouth. Then he says, "I know that you can't right now, and that's fine, I'll take whatever you're willing to give me, because it's you that I want more than anything, Vanessa. Just you."

"When you say things like that you make it impossible for me to leave, you know that, right?"

With a chuckle, he says, "I think that's the point."

Then he lowers his head and starts to kiss me unhurriedly; my head tilts to give him better access when his tongue touches mine. I loop my arms around his neck to keep him close to me and to feel every part of his body perfectly fit against mine. I sense myself falling for him even more with every stroke of his tongue, with every change in pressure of his lips, and with every emotion that he delivers in this kiss.

My eyes are still closed when he breaks the kiss, and when I open them he's already letting me go while taking a step away from me. I instantly miss his lips, his tenderness . . . and him.

Without saying a word, he shoves his hands in his jeans pockets and looks on as I open the car door. Just when I'm about to climb into the driver's seat, I look up again at Cameron, whose dark eyes are clouded with an unspoken question.

Do you really still want this?

This time, I take the easy out and don't answer.

CHAPTER TWENTY-FIVE

Saturday comes much quicker than I want it to.

And when it's finally here, I want it over before it even begins.

I spoke with my attorney again yesterday afternoon, and she reassured me that everything was going to be all right. That possibly, if this works out today, Matthew may be willing to drop his petition for paternity since there really isn't a question as to whether or not he's Josie's father. But that would mean that there would have to be some sort of visitation worked out, and of course, as my attorney made sure to point out several times, child support.

I'm not sure how I feel about all of that yet, even the child support. Because I've been able raise Josie without his help and I don't want to have him think that I can't going forward. However, I'm not an idiot and would definitely consider it. Again, this would all depend on a lot of variables going extraordinarily well today. So I won't hold my breath.

Josie is taking this all in stride, which further proves how much more mature and evolved she is than her own mother. She's sitting in the living room with a book in her lap, her eyes scanning the page for something in particular, and seems at peace with whatever the outcome is today.

That helps to relax me as the time approaches for Matthew's arrival, which should be any minute now. In those ten minutes, I find myself hoping that he doesn't disappoint her in any way, that what he said in his initial letter is exactly what he intends to do.

When the doorbell rings, my heart literally feels as if it drops all the way down to my feet and then boomerangs up to my throat, where I know it will stay lodged for the remainder of the afternoon. Josie stands up quickly and heads for the door. I meet her there, and as I reach for doorknob, she says, "Wait, Mom. Give me a second, okay?"

She pulls some of her blonde hair behind her ears and then runs her hands down the front of the skirt she's wearing, ensuring the pleats in the fabric are nice and neat. Then she looks up at me one more time and nods. "Okay, I'm ready."

Leaning down, I kiss her forehead and tell her I love her before finally opening the door to her father.

He looks exactly the same.

From the glint in his bright blue eyes to the innocent but knowing smile he wears on his face. Of course, with age, he also looks more distinguished, but that face . . . I swear I feel as if I've been transported back to that very day we met on campus.

"Hello, Vanessa," he says cordially and nicely enough that I don't feel put off by him instantly. Then his eyes quickly scan down to where Josie is standing beside me, the top of her head just reaching my shoulder, and he stares at her with complete wonderment in his eyes. "You must be Josie."

"And you must be my dad." She steps forward, sticks out her hand, and says, "It's nice to finally meet you."

Matthew looks to me for approval, and I nod, so he takes her hand in his and shakes it formally. "I can't begin to tell you how nice it is to finally meet you too, Josie."

"Why don't you come in and have a seat so we can all talk?" I offer politely.

Josie lets him go, and he follows us into the living room, where she sits next to me, and Matthew takes the opposite seat, still staring at her.

"I'm sorry, I don't mean to gawk, but it's like—"

"Like looking in a mirror," I finish for him. "She does look a lot like you, Matthew. I've always thought that too."

"I see you in her too, Vanessa. She's so . . . I'm sorry." He looks to Josie again and then says, "*You* are so beautiful."

"Thank you." Both Josie and I say this at the same exact time.

She looks to me, and I sense a relief in her so deep that it overwhelms me. I thought I could hold it together, but seeing her like this, I start to get emotional, and that's the last thing I want to do in front of either of them. So I excuse myself to the bathroom to collect myself.

Looking at myself in the bathroom mirror, I wipe my eyes quickly before any mascara starts to run over. Then I say to myself as calmly and quietly as possible, "Vanessa, get your ass back in there and be there for your daughter. You can do this."

Taking a deep, cleansing breath, I open the door and walk back down the hallway, where I hear a snippet of their conversation.

"So how are you doing in school? You should be in high school now, right? A freshman, I think."

"Next year I'll be a freshman. This is my last year of junior high school, and I do okay."

"Something tells me that you're probably an honor roll student," Matthew says and guesses right.

Josie doesn't say anything, but from the smirk on her face, he figures it out. "How about friends? I bet you have a lot of them."

"I have two best friends: Carrie and Lorelei, and they're awesome. For Halloween this year we all dressed up as the Teenage Mutant Ninja Turtles."

There is a pregnant pause in the conversation, then Matthew clears his throat and asks her if there is anything she wants to know about him.

"Everything," Josie admits.

"Okay, well, I'm married and oh, you have two little sisters, twins actually."

I can tell from where I'm hiding in the hallway that Josie is grinning wide when she says, "I read that in your letter. What do they look like?"

I hear a ruffling of movement and take the chance to come out of the shadows, so to speak, and sit down again. "Is everything okay, kid?" I ask Josie quietly, running my hand down the length of her hair soothingly.

"Yeah, my dad was just showing me pictures of my little sisters. Do you want to see too?"

"I'm not sure your mom wants to just yet, Josie," Matthew interjects.

I'll give him credit, he knows that as much as I'm sitting here and giving in to this meeting, he realizes that with the history between us—and not just where Josie is concerned—I may not be fully ready to see the other part of his life. But I want to make sure he knows without a shadow of a doubt that he has never and never will get the best of me.

"Of course I want to see," I say, making Josie smile and Matthew a little uncomfortable for the first time since he's arrived.

What he shows me on his phone is a picture of two beautiful baby girls, both of them dressed the same in tiny pink tutus over plain pink onesies. They both have very fine blonde hair, and their eyes are as blue as their father's and Josie's.

"They're beautiful, Matthew," I say and hand him back his phone. "What are their names?"

"Isabella and Sophia." He smiles, glancing at the picture once more before putting away his phone. "They're just learning how to walk."

"Mom, how awesome is it that I have not one but two sisters?"

I kiss the crown of Josie's head and agree that it's awesome, because what can I say? No, it's not, it's completely unfair that this man missed that part of your life and yet he can sit here with a smile in front of us? I can't. I have to bite my tongue, as I will probably be doing for the rest of this conversation.

"Do you think I can meet them someday?" Josie asks both of us.

"We'll see," I say at the same time that Matthew says, "Sure."

I laugh and then say to Josie, "We just need to work things out, sweetie, okay?"

Then I realize that I may be cramping the conversation that had been flowing so well between the two of them while I was gone, and that kind of makes me feel bad for Josie. So I politely excuse myself again and let them both know that maybe they can get to know each other a little better if I'm not in the room.

"I'll be in the art studio if you need me, okay?"

When she agrees, I walk to my studio, where I begin pacing the room back and forth for the next twenty minutes. I leave the door open so I can hear a laugh or a giggle every so often between them, but I don't eavesdrop this time. It's not until I hear Josie call for me that I come back downstairs and see them standing by the front door.

"Thank you for letting me meet you, Josie. I hope we can do this again," Matthew says to her and puts out his hand for her to shake.

"I hope so too," she says. And with the inflection of happiness in her voice, I know she means it.

Honestly, I'm happy for her. But I can't lie and say that it makes this any easier. Then again, this isn't about me; this is about her. So I go with it.

"I guess we need to talk," I say to Matthew and he agrees. "Josie, do you mind going to your room, and I'll be up in a few minutes?"

She says good-bye to him and runs off, leaving us alone for the first time.

"I don't know where to start," he says sheepishly.

"How about the beginning?"

Then I think, no, I don't need answers for the past anymore. "Actually, forget about that. It's done. What I *do* want to know for sure before anything else moves forward is that you won't screw up with her again. Because I swear, if you do, I will hunt you down and kill you with my bare hands."

Matthew tries to keep his face from breaking out into a smile.

"I'm serious, Matthew. That little girl has been wondering her whole life about you and I won't let you mess with her head."

"I'm not smiling because I think it's funny. I'm smiling because I knew that you would take care of her and raise her to be the best, most amazing person she could be . . . and she is." He stops and thinks of what he's going to say next carefully. "You've done an incredible job, Vanessa, and there are not enough words in the English language for me to ever say thank you properly."

I don't really have much to say to that and didn't know until right then that I even wanted to hear all of that come from his mouth. It doesn't excuse his behavior and nonexistence all these years, but it's the right step that he needed to take with me.

"I know my track record with you and Josie isn't worth a thing—and I deserve that and more—but I really want to try to be something to her. It may take years, and I'm prepared for it to take that long, but I mean it."

I expel a rush of breath as my heart beats wildly. "Matthew, the only way that we can even start considering that is if you drop the petition immediately."

After a brief second when I catch him off guard, he says, "I agree. I'll call my attorney immediately."

Now it's my turn to be caught off guard. Because I didn't expect him to agree so readily to my request to drop the petition. But it's not enough, so I keep going. "And if you think you'll be added to the birth certificate, you're crazy. First of all, you've never been a father to her, so for me to even consider doing that, you will have to prove yourself much more to me and Josie."

"I plan to do just that, Vanessa."

"Matthew, if you think simply saying that out loud is going to be—"

"It's not enough, I know that. I intend to be the man I should have been years ago to you and to our daughter. You deserve that, of course. But that beautiful little girl deserves it more than anyone. I realize that it's difficult for you to believe me or trust me, but all I need from you right now is to at least be open . . . even if just a little bit, and that will be enough for now."

As much as I want to say no and keep on hating him, I can't. For my daughter's sake, I have to make an effort. It kills me to admit it to myself, but he's right. I have to try and trust him.

Reluctantly, I say to him, "You're right, Matthew. I'll try."

"Thank you, Vanessa."

He leaves then, and when I close the door behind him, I lean against it, closing my eyes and thinking that I didn't consider it would be that easy to convince him to drop the petition. That doesn't mean that I still won't have my guard up where he's concerned, and I probably always will . . . but it's a start.

CHAPTER TWENTY-SIX

"I t really went that well?"

This is coming from Julia, who has asked me that same question about a dozen times in the five minutes I've been in their house later that same night. Josie had promised to babysit for them earlier in the week, so I had to stop by here to drop her off.

"Seriously? Like you didn't gut him like a fish or anything?" she asks while tidying up the kitchen. And then she freezes when a thought occurs to her. "Wait a second. I'm not going to see anything about you on the ten o'clock news, am I? Because I have to admit, that might be a little awesome."

"No, no, and no," I say.

"So then everything worked out for the best and Josie seems okay with it?" Alex asks, after shooting a confused look to his wife.

We all look to where Josie is helping Violet color some pieces of paper on the floor in the family room, out of earshot.

"I think so," I say and turn to face them. "I have a feeling that she would have said something to me if it wasn't okay."

"Then what's next?" Alex asks.

I run through the preliminary details, having spoken to my attorney again this afternoon after Matthew left. And in fact, he had already spoken to his and asked for the petition to be dropped. Now it's just a question of working out visitation and perhaps child support.

"What do you mean, 'perhaps child support'?" Julia asks with a face that looks like her eyebrows could not possibly go any higher if she tried. "Girlie, if you don't make that motherf—"

"Stop. Please. Don't. I get it, Julia, and thank you so very much for the reminder," I say to her. "I need to think about it a little more because I've been fine all this time and I don't know . . . I feel like it makes me look like that's all I care about. Is that weird?"

"Yes," from Julia and a no from my brother.

They look at each other, and she squints her eyes at him, trying her hardest to look evil, which makes him chuckle and blow her off completely. "Listen," he says, "so long as you and Josie are happy, I'm sure that part of it will work itself out."

"It better," Julia mumbles underneath her breath.

I get up to leave after saying good-bye to Josie and letting her know that I'll be back to pick her up by eleven o'clock. In my head I'm thinking that I'll just drive straight home and . . .

And do what exactly?

I'm not in the mood to paint. Actually, I'm too moody to paint or draw or work on any of the unfinished pieces I have in my studio at the moment. So what am I going to do? Sit around and twiddle my thumbs?

Then an idea pops into my head, and before I can chicken out, I jump into my car and drive straight to Cameron's house. In the twenty or so minutes it takes me to get there, I start having second thoughts. But then I convince myself that I should just keep driving, so I do.

When I reach his street, I stop midway and pull over, putting my car in park and staring down the rest of the road that leads to his driveway, wondering if I'm doing the right thing here.

Stop it, Vanessa, just drive, I tell myself.

I finally make it to his house and park next to his car but just end up sitting in my own car again. It's as if my body is stuck to this seat and there is no way I can get out. I try to rack my brain to figure out what the hell is wrong with me. Why can't I go that extra step here? Then my cell phone buzzes in my purse.

I dig through and see that it's Cameron calling. Well, if there ever was a sign, which I don't necessarily believe in, this is it.

"Hello," I say into the phone. "I was just thinking about you."

"That's funny, because so was I. Well, obviously I was since I dialed your number and we're talking and stuff," he says. Then he's quiet for a second again. "I'm sorry, I'm rambling, aren't I?"

I smile into the phone, picturing him rubbing the back of his neck as a nervous reflex while he's talking to me. "You were a little bit, yes, but that's okay."

"You make me a little nervous," he says. "And as I've already told you, I'm not very good at this."

I think back to all the times we've seen each other, and everything else in between, and wonder how in the world he can possibly think this about himself. Then I wonder why the hell I'm sitting here still in the car when I can be seeing him in person just a few steps away.

"So how did it go today?" he asks suddenly, changing the subject.

I was getting ready to get out of the car when he asks this of me. For some reason, his concern switches on something inside of me. It's so hard to explain, but it's as if my brain comes to a sudden realization that I should stop this before it goes any further . . . even though it's already gone much further than I expected with Cameron. But my heart starts to pound in my chest like a bass drum as I battle with this right outside his door and in his driveway of all places.

If it were any other time in my life—free of stress and without having to worry about making sure everything keeps going smoothly with Josie and her father—I'd be okay, I think. But I can't seem to let go of the fact that she still needs me. And in order for me to be there for her, I must be able to focus on her. With Cameron in the picture, I don't think that I can do that to the best of my abilities, and I owe that to my daughter after messing up so badly up to this point.

Maybe these are all stupid excuses for me simply being afraid of getting hurt again. Because if Cameron and I move to the next step, and the step beyond that, and it doesn't work out, then it's not only me I have to be concerned about getting hurt . . . it's Josie too.

And I can't let that happen.

"It went fine," I say to him. "Really well, actually."

"That's good to hear. I'm happy for you and for Josie."

A long silence stretches between us. Then he asks, "Is it too soon to ask when I can see you again?"

"Cameron—"

"I was wondering because—"

"Wait a second, I need to say something and I need to say it now before I change my mind."

"Sure, sure, sorry about that."

God, why does he have to be so nice? It makes this that much more difficult. And then I smile to myself, thinking of how he was worried about me calling him nice in the past, since nice guys always finish last. Sadly, he was right in this case, and now I'm convinced I'm the world's worst person.

"Listen, Cameron," I say with trepidation thick in my throat. "My daughter really needs me right now, and I think it would be best if we take time to think things over."

I hear his steady breathing on the line, so I know he's still there. Probably questioning why he ever decided to date me in the first place; probably wishing he'd chosen the cupcake lady after all. After a few seconds of radio silence, I ask, "Can you say something?"

"We're breaking up, right?" he asks, more to himself, I think, so I don't answer. "I mean, that's essentially what you're saying to me. Because, let me get this straight, it's not the right time for you?"

I guess when you break it down, yes, that's exactly what I'm saying. And yup, it sounds as awful in my head as it does when he says it like that to me.

"Vanessa, can I ask you something? When will it ever be the right time for you? Because if you think life will ever get easier, it won't. Sometimes you have to take a chance . . . this is one of those times, because I know that you feel more than just simple attraction between us, that there is something here worth investing the time in."

He's right about that part . . . I did feel it, I still do. But it's also a little scary to me, the not knowing what's going to happen. I've been able to live my life for so long with just worrying about one person that I don't think I can handle much else, especially right now . . . or ever. Maybe all those jokes I've made to Josie about starting to date when I get into an old folks' home aren't jokes at all but what's really in store for me.

"So I don't have any say in this?" he asks while I'm sitting here silent and having a mini meltdown parked in his driveway. "Because I say we should see where this takes us, Vanessa."

"I want to, Cameron, I really do, but—"

"But what? You just said so yourself: you want to."

"But it's not enough, not right now," I say, and with that he's the one to go quiet again. "Cameron, it wouldn't be fair to you or to us." After a long pause, and with nothing coming from his end, I say softly, "I'm sorry. I wish things could be different, I really do. But I just can't right now."

"So there's nothing else left to say, is there?"

"No, I guess not."

I put the car in reverse and slowly and ever so quietly roll down his driveway without Cameron ever knowing how close I am to him right now. It's not until I get to the end of the street that I hang up, since neither of us wants to say good-bye.

CHAPTER TWENTY-SEVEN

It took a while, but after a few weeks of back and forth between our attorneys, Matthew and I come up with a plausible visitation schedule and child support arrangement, which Julia is way too excited over. I haven't decided yet on legal paternity, but, much to my own surprise, I haven't ruled it out. Matthew has been holding up his side of the bargain, so we'll see about that part later on . . . much later.

Josie has been adjusting nicely and seems genuinely happy to have her father in her life. She's been seeing him once a week after school and one day each weekend so far. Matthew has been sticking to his word by calling Josie every night and hasn't canceled once on any of their scheduled visits. The only unknown they haven't breached yet is Josie meeting her stepmother and two little sisters. But that will finally be happening today, when Matthew picks her up in a little while to spend the whole day with his family. No sleepover, because *I'm* not there yet. And until I am, that's not happening.

I'm running through my list of errands I have to run while she's with her dad today when Josie appears in front of me. She's sporting a cute red and blue striped summer top and a pair of jean shorts; her blonde hair is up in a high ponytail, and on her feet are a pair of my old black Havaianas, which makes me smile.

"How do I look?"

"Adorable, of course."

She twirls around and then asks again.

"Sweetie, you look perfect. Why are you so worried about how you look anyway?"

She shrugs as if it's not a big deal and says, "Just want to look nice."

"Are you sure that's it?"

I watch her face for any reaction, and then I see it; she's worried about making a good first impression with Matthew's family. God, I love this kid. She has such a good heart, and the fact that she's so eager to make this first impression go well shows me that she's really trying to make this relationship with her father work.

"I guarantee you that it will be fine, okay?" She agrees halfheartedly. So I say, "Listen, kid, I think you're the best, and anybody who doesn't think that is crazy. End of story. So don't worry about it. Just be yourself and you'll do great and they will love you, I promise."

"You really think so, Mom?"

"I know it, kid."

She looks much more like her usual carefree self for a second, until her nose scrunches up, reminding me of her father, as it has done for years, but now I can freely tell her so. "What's wrong now?"

"I have to tell you something, but you have to promise you won't get mad."

"By the laws set forth in the parents' commandments, that statement can never be agreed to by any parent, as they reserve the right to judgment after hearing whatever it is that their offspring will say after it is prefaced with that statement."

"What did you just say?" she asks, completely bewildered.

"I said I can't make that promise so just spit it out."

We both crane our necks at the sound of Matthew's car pulling into our driveway.

"You better hurry up and tell me whatever it is you have on your mind before your father gets to that door."

Josie starts to walk backward slowly toward the door, and when she reaches it, she says, in a run-on sentence one-breath rush, "I signed up for the science fair that Mr. Thomas is having at school next week before Christmas break and I want you to come and not chicken out because he's going to be there and that weird cupcake lady will probably be there too and she's really been hanging around a lot lately again because you're not around and I just wanted to see if there is any way that you would think of getting back together with Mr. Thomas because you guys were really supercute together and even my friends think so, and that's it."

The doorbell rings and she turns to open the door.

"Hi, Dad!" Then she turns around to me and says, "Bye, Mom!"

And then she's out the door with Matthew before he even gets a chance to say much of anything other than hello and good-bye to me.

The little sneak.

I start to laugh out loud at what she was able to expel in one breath and with such conviction, no less, before leaving. And then I laugh even more, thinking of exactly what she said, especially the "weird cupcake lady" part. Because, really, she's kind of weird. I mean, who goes around wearing so many variations of brown almost every single day of the year? I happen to love certain colors in my wardrobe too, but you don't see me wearing all black, all day, every day, three hundred sixty-five days of the year. That would be weird . . . very weird. And besides, I already did that back in high school when I obsessed over Depeche Mode and the Cure.

I'll definitely have to have a talk with Josie about this more than I already have, which really wasn't much to begin with. I simply told her that it wasn't the right time for me to be dating.

She had the same reaction as Cameron . . . not good.

What she actually said was that I was being stupid and then proceeded to ask me what I was doing at that exact moment that had me so busy that I couldn't make time for him.

To say that I felt outwitted by my own daughter would be putting it mildly. But she's kind of right. The problem is that I don't have the nerve to fix this with Cameron. And what if he doesn't want to talk to me?

He texted me a handful of times just to say hello and that he'd been thinking of me, then stopped after I didn't respond; it feels terrible not to answer him.

If I were him, and I called after these last few weeks of not even a word, I wouldn't want to talk to me either. So no matter what, I'm back to square one.

"Would you listen to yourself?" I say out loud to nobody but me. "You sound like an annoying . . . girl."

The truth of it is, I do miss him, and I miss that beginning part of our relationship where I was finding out all these interesting things about him and letting him know all the little things about me that I never tell anyone; it's this perfect little bubble that we can never get back to. And the sex . . . for the one night I spent with him, I don't think I'll ever get over that. He was perfect; gentle and assuring, warm and safe . . . everything I didn't realize I wanted or needed. I even miss those T-shirts of his, because they always looked so damn cute on him. And that is probably the most attractive thing about him: that he doesn't realize how gorgeous and sexy he is.

So what the hell am I doing about it?

Nothing.

But I still have to go to Josie's science fair . . . not alone though, so I call for reinforcements.

Alex picks up on the second ring, asking if everything is okay.

"Yeah, why wouldn't it be?" I ask him.

"Isn't today the day that Josie meets Matthew's family?"

"Yes, she left a little while ago, but that's not why I'm calling you."

He tells me to hang on a second. Then I hear him in the background telling Violet that she needs to get down from whatever limb she's hanging off of in their house. I'm awful, because I start to laugh at this.

"It's not funny, Vanessa," he says in a frustrated voice. "She's been climbing this empty bookcase that I have in my office like a freaking monkey every time I turn my back."

"It's a little funny." My laughter dies down long enough that I can tell him the real reason for my call. "Josie has this science fair thing that she just told me about next week. I was wondering if you wouldn't mind coming with me."

"I'll be there." He says Violet's name sternly again and then comes back to me. "Listen, I have to go before she breaks something here, so just text me the details and I'll meet you there, okay?"

"Sounds good."

When I hang up, the errand list is forgotten about completely. Instead, I head upstairs to my art studio and sit down on my stool. I stare at the blank canvas, thinking of all the ways I can fill the empty space, all the limitless possibilities waiting to be fleshed out by my hands.

But nothing ever comes, and all I'm left with is what I started with . . . a blank and lonely looking canvas.

CHAPTER TWENTY-EIGHT

When I pull into the school parking lot the following week for the science fair, it's almost full to capacity. But I don't see Alex's car anywhere, so I shoot him a quick text before walking inside and straight to the gym, where I'm supposed to meet up with him and find Josie's entry.

Standing at the door of the gym, I peek inside and try to find my brother in case I missed his car outside, but I can't spot him anywhere in the crowd. However, I do see Cameron.

He's looking right at me with those dark eyes of his from across the room. He's wearing one of his Professor Indiana Jones suits and looks too good to be true, reminding me of the very first time I saw him on that Back to School Night. He even has his cute little wire-rimmed glasses on. And then he pushes them up the bridge of his nose as if to distract himself and darts his eyes to another part of the gym, forgetting about me.

I deserve it, but it still hurts.

I start to look around again, but this time for Josie. She never told me what her entry was, so I'm curious to see what she's been working on in secret after school.

I'm almost at her table when I feel a tug on the bottom of my skirt. It's Violet.

"Aunt Nessa," she says in a sleepy voice. "What are you doing here?"

I bend down and pick her up. She instantly rubs her eyes and puts her head down on my shoulder.

Before I can ask what's going on, I look up and see Julia coming my way with a diaper bag strapped across her chest and a frustrated look on her face. "Oh good, you found Aunt Vanessa."

"Where is Alex? I thought he was coming," I ask her.

"Daddy had to go to emergency, Aunt Nessa," Violet says, sounding less sleepy.

"What happened?" This I ask of Julia, who is trying to extract Violet from my arms.

After she hitches her on to her hip, she clarifies, "He didn't *go* to emergency. He *had* an emergency at work. Which makes no sense to me because how the hell does an art gallery have an emergency? It's a freaking art gallery. Did he run out of paint?" She takes a much-needed breath and then says, "Anyway, he sent me instead. But this one"—she nods to Violet, who is rubbing her eyes again—"was in the middle of a nap, so yeah, it's been really fun."

"He didn't have to call you, but thanks for coming."

"No problem."

"Yeah, I can see that," I say with a laugh.

"So where's Josie?" She looks around the room and spots Cameron first. "Oooh, there's your man."

"He is not my man, and please don't you dare make me regret telling my brother that I liked you enough and gave him my stamp of approval before he asked you to marry him."

"Technically, we did this," she says and swings Violet around in a semicircle. "Before doing that, so it wouldn't have mattered what you said to him anyway. So there."

"Real mature."

"Ditto."

We're both laughing through this, and Violet starts to giggle, that beautiful little noise that only a toddler can make. But once we stop laughing, I say to Julia in a deadpan voice, "Seriously, do not say a word about it."

She makes a face, and I can't tell if she's letting me know she's not going to say a word about it or if she plans to give a diatribe on the subject to anyone who will listen. "My lips are sealed . . . in protest, but sealed nonetheless."

"Thank you very—"

The cupcake lady in all her brown-toned, coordinated attire interrupts us, and of course, she's holding a tray of cupcakes, because why wouldn't she be?

"You must be Ms. Holt, Josie's mother," she says with an air of pompousness.

"Yes, that's right." I put on the most fake smile I can muster. "And you are?"

"I'm Christopher's mother." She looks past my shoulder to a table where her son is proudly standing with his entry and talking with some of his friends. "That's him right there."

"You must be so proud," Julia chimes in. "His entry looks pretty awesome."

It really does. From here it looks to be a volcano that goes off, and lava comes pouring down the sides of his homemade mountain.

Cupcake Lady's judging eyes go up and down Julia with a look of disdain, as if she can't be bothered. Then she says, "Yes, it is . . . awesome."

Here we go. I'm waiting for Julia to go off on this woman, but then I remember that Violet is here, so she's probably seething with rage and biting her tongue. I glance over at Julia, and yeah, she is most definitely dying to say something, but she keeps it in check. Thank God.

Cupcake Lady leans in to say something only to me, catching me off guard. "I heard about things not working out so well with you and Mr. Thomas. Such a shame." She backs away with an almost evil smile on her face. "Don't you worry, dear, I'll make sure he's well taken care of."

"Did you just call me 'dear'? I think only my mother calls me that."

"Okay, that's enough, Count Chocula," Julia says and steps in between us. "Mind your business and get to steppin'."

Her face still has that really weird, scary smile on it as she walks away. We keep our eyes on her, tracking her all the way until she approaches Cameron with her terrible tasting cupcakes, which he of course refuses.

With a raised eyebrow, I turn to Julia, who looks like she's ready to kill someone. "Seriously? Get to steppin'? Are we in a TLC music video that I don't know about?"

"I couldn't think of anything else to say that didn't involve me using words that would make me fill up Violet's swear jar and then some. Sorry."

"Mommy, I'm tired," Violet says through a yawn. "And hungry."

Julia puts her down so she can rifle through the diaper bag for some snacks. Then Julia springs up with a devilish grin on her face. Taking Violet's hand in hers, she says, "Come with Mommy, let's go look at the cool things here while I look for snacks, okay?"

When they leave to walk around the gym, I finally spot Josie and make a beeline to her table.

"Hey, sweetie, this looks great!"

It really does and I am so impressed with her. She has this giant white poster board propped up with all these different steps, and at the very end is a small desk fan that is actually blowing out shaved ice over her table in a cascade . . . or snow, which is why her entry is named How to Make Snow.

Before Josie can say a single word, there's a loud crash to our left, followed by a huge splat, which is then followed by some yelling from Cupcake Lady herself. I close my eyes, because I can only imagine what my sister-in-law just did and would much rather continue imagining it rather than seeing it with my own eyes.

To Josie, I say, "Please tell me that Julia isn't involved."

Josie giggles through her answer. "No . . . but Violet is."

That's when I open my eyes to see Cupcake Lady's cupcakes splattered on the ground and her face frozen in horror. Then I see Violet walking toward me, splotches of cupcake icing adorning her once adorable little floral swing top and leggings, with a huge smile on her face, licking each finger clean. She's holding her mother's hand, and Julia has a huge smile to match her daughter's.

"What happened?" I ask.

"Mommy said that she found my snacks underneath the cupcake tray."

"Now, Violet, I didn't say to pull the tray from the table though, did I? That would have been silly of Mommy to say."

Violet looks up to her mother, who brings her finger to her mouth to shush her. "I'm still hungry, Mommy."

"Baby girl, for that, I'll take you to Swensen's right now and let you order the yummiest, most ginormous ice cream sundae that you've ever seen."

And with the biggest squeal of delight I've ever heard from Violet, they say their good-byes and head off to plot another take-down, God knows where, but I bet it will be on the news tonight.

"I can't believe she did that. That woman is nuts."

"Vanessa."

That voice and the way he says my name send a thrill down my spine. He's standing right behind me, so I turn around slowly, not sure of how this is going to go.

"Hello, Mr. Thomas."

"We're really back to that, are we?" he asks, with a hint of playfulness in his voice.

Leaning forward, I whisper, "Well, I can't very well call you Cameron in front of everyone, it would be inappropriate."

"Guess what?" he whispers right back. "You just did."

We're still standing way too close to each other, close enough that I feel the brush of his stubble against my cheek when he leans in and says to me, "You weren't even going to say hello to me, were you?"

Then he steps back as if remembering where we are and that we aren't together anymore. As he runs a hand through his hair in frustration, he adds, "Sorry, you don't have to answer that. I guess I'm still . . . adjusting." He pushes his eyeglasses up the bridge of his nose again. "But seeing you again is . . ."

"Like a bad dream?" I offer up as a suggestion.

His lips curl up a little in a grin. "No, not at all, Vanessa. I was going to say that seeing you again is like a breath of fresh air."

"Oh."

I don't have anything to say to that and feel like a fool. He still wants me. I thought that might be true but wasn't totally sure. Inside of me, my stomach does that little flip-flop it does as I imagine what it would be like to be even closer to him, to be able to touch him, to have him inside of me, and *with* me all over again. Instead, I'm just standing here in front of him with nothing to add to this conversation because I can't bring myself to rectify things between us.

"Well . . . it was really a pleasure to see you again." He sounds more like his professional teacher persona already and then looks over my shoulder at Josie. "Josie, great job with the snow maker. It's one of my favorite entries here today."

"Thanks for helping me with it, Mr. Thomas. It was so cool."

"You're welcome," he says to her, then directs his attention back to me. "Good-bye, Vanessa."

It's not until he's already turning on his heel and his back is to me that I can manage to say good-bye back to him. He doesn't turn around again, and for the rest of the time that I'm standing there frozen to that spot on the gym floor, he still doesn't grace me with his dark gaze. But I keep my eyes trained on him as he maneuvers his way through the crowd and stops by each entry, taking the time to introduce himself to the parents and to acknowledge the hard work done by each of his students.

"Earth to Mom, come in, Mom," Josie says and bumps shoulders with me. "I feel it is my duty as your daughter to tell you that you kind of look pathetic right now."

"Well, that's not a very nice thing to say to your own mother."

She puts her hand on her hip and raises an eyebrow as if to challenge me further. I roll my eyes and say, "Yeah, maybe you're right. Thanks for the heads-up, kid."

"He still likes you and asks about you every so often, Mom."

"Really?"

"Yup. And if I were you, I would totally go for it."

"Josie, I already told you—"

"Yeah, you did, and I still don't get it." She puffs some hair away from her forehead, looking beyond frustrated with me, then mumbles, "Never mind, Mom."

Well, this whole day has worked out great.

With the exception of the Cupcake Lady getting hers, this day has gone to hell in a handbag really quick. And after the fair, we end up going home and having a bite to eat for dinner—all of this done in almost complete silence, with the exception of a handful of yeahs and nos from Josie, who is now not even talking to me. I go to bed frustrated beyond belief with myself.

I toss and turn for what feels like hours, only the flickering light from the television changing programming against the walls as my companion. At around two o'clock in the morning, I sit up and take my cell phone off the nightstand and contemplate calling Cameron. But what would I say? Would saying sorry and admitting I made a terrible mistake be enough?

Defeated and unsure, I toss the phone on the comforter instead and fall back against the pillows.

CHAPTER TWENTY-NINE

Are you seriously still not talking to me?" I ask Josie as I drive her to school the next morning.

We're about to arrive at her school when I lower the volume on the morning talk radio station I was listening to. I found myself getting so exasperated sitting right next to her with not even a word spoken the whole way here.

She doesn't even acknowledge what I asked her. I look over to her as I'm turning into the drop-off area and catch her watching me and then quickly averting her eyes toward the passenger-side window.

"Josie, I've told you before, it's not a good time for—"

"I heard you the first hundred times, Mom," she finally blurts out in frustration. "Just drop me off here."

"Wait a second," I say to her while she's already opening the door. "I need to talk to you about this."

Standing outside of the car, she slams the door shut, and I don't miss the look on her face that says she has no intention of continuing this conversation.

Angry tapping on my window makes me almost jump right out of my seat. Turning to look at who it is, I see the same volunteer parent patroling the drop-off area.

As I lower my window, she says to me in a very annoyed voice, "Lady, you need get to moving, you're holding up the line."

Smiling, I say as nicely as possible, "Yes, but I need to talk with my daughter for a moment longer."

"Move it."

"Just give me a second," I say and turn to see Josie already walking away with the throng of students making their way inside the school. "Shit," I mumble underneath my breath, even more frustrated now because I can barely find Josie's head in the crowd.

"Lady, if you don't move this car, I will—"

"You'll do what, exactly?! You'll put me in drop-off area jail?!" I put the car in park and get out.

"You cannot leave your car here, ma'am!" she shouts, but I'm already speed walking to catch up to Josie.

I'm shouting out her name when I get to the entrance of the building, and a security guard stops me from coming in. "Please, I just need to talk my daughter for a second. She's right . . . there!" I spot her staring at me in complete mortification, flanked by Carrie and Lorelei. Waving my arms up in the air, I yell, "Josie!"

She reluctantly starts walking to me, clutching the straps of her backpack and dragging her feet the entire way. "See, here she comes," I say, smiling to the security guard, who nods then lets Josie through to come back outside to me.

There is still a bunch of kids making their way into the building, so I grab her upper arm and gently move over to the side of the building, where we won't be in the way of the crowd.

She crosses her arms and keeps her head down. I'm not sure if it's because she is embarrassed or disinterested. A part of me wants to shake her to make her get over my decision about Cameron, which I obviously won't do. There is another part of me that *needs* to make her understand that it was the best decision at the time. She doesn't need to know that I already regret it and wish I could take it back. But it's too late now. It's done.

"Listen, Josie," I say to her calmly. "I've gone over this with you already. Maybe I wasn't clear, so I'll say it again."

"Don't bother, Mom." Her bright blue eyes peek through her bangs for a second, then she drops her gaze again. "I don't need you to explain it to me again. I'm not stupid."

"I never said you were, sweetie."

"No, you didn't," she agrees. "But you also don't think I don't know what it is you're doing all over again."

"What do you mean, 'all over again'?"

Picking her head up and meeting my eyes, she says, "You're using me as an excuse . . . again, and sorry, Mom, but that's messed up! Because—and this may be hard for you to accept—I don't need you to do that for me anymore . . . I'm fine! And if I'm not fine, I *will* be fine eventually! So please just stop using me as the excuse, because it's not me. It's you!"

Whoa.

I'm speechless, because she's one hundred percent right. I've been using her as my excuse for . . . geez, not just Cameron, but a lot of things in my life. It's like she's my go-to crutch when I need her to be. She's obviously beyond being fed up about it . . . and I don't blame her one bit.

"I—"

"Can I go now? The bell is about to ring," she says and looks behind her.

The crowd is almost completely gone by the entrance now, which means that yes, the bell signaling first period is about to go off any second. I don't say anything to her; I can't bring myself to yet. So I nod my head, letting her know that yes she can go, and she does, making it in time to cross the threshold as the shrill bell goes off loudly in the background.

Standing there too stunned and disappointed in myself for doing exactly what she said, I mentally catalog all the little things I've ever used Josie as an excuse for, like my nonexistent social life and not pursuing a career in the arts, until reaching the top one on the list to date: Cameron.

Granted, thinking that she needs me to be there for her should be the very first thought of any parent, but this goes well beyond that. Because deep down, I know that it has nothing to do with worrying about being there for her, or making it look like I'm a responsible person to her, or making sure that she's well taken care of . . . all of those are a given where our relationship is concerned. When I dig down even deeper, I realize it's my fear of dating again and possibly being hurt that makes me use Josie as a cop-out.

Okay, get yourself together, Vanessa, I think to myself as I slowly come to terms with this. Eventually the fog lifts from my brain, and I start to walk back to my car with my head down, avoiding the inquisitive eyes of a handful of students who are still milling around the entrance. But my car isn't there. I look up and down the drop-off area just in time to catch a glimpse of a tow truck pulling my car down the main road and onto the highway.

"Wait! That's my car!" I yell.

I start to run but then stop when I know that there is no way I'm going to catch up to it. That's when I realize just how screwed I am, because in that car is my purse, which has my cell phone in it to call someone to pick me up.

"I told you not to park there, lady." This comes from behind me.

Without turning around, I already know it's the volunteer parent who mans the drop-off area having a serious gloating moment.

Great, just great. Now I'm going to have to eat crow, big-time.

I turn around slowly, and with the biggest smile I can possibly come up with, I ask, "Can I borrow your phone, please?"

CHAPTER THIRTY

Life is all about the moments that make up the big picture. Sometimes those moments can be as big and vast as a clear blue sky on a bright, sunny day. And sometimes those moments can be so tiny and unremarkable that they slip through your fingers before you realize they will come to mean something to you greater than you ever imagined.

I've learned the hard way that I need to take those moments as they come and try to shape them into what they're meant to be. Because a lesson learned once doesn't give me the right to make the same mistake over and over. No matter how silly or trivial the mistake is, I need to fix it right then and there and move on.

Take Josie and me, for instance . . .

After having one of the craziest times of our lives—a lot of that crazy belongs squarely on my shoulders, which I can now admit with no hesitation—we can look back as we face the new year ahead and laugh. Because it's kind of funny when I think about it.

Especially that day a couple of weeks ago at her school. It makes Josie and everyone else in my family crack up when they bring up the tow truck and how I was put in drop-off area jail for a day. No, not a real jail, but with my car gone, it certainly felt like that.

And a lesson was learned there. Not the obvious one that I shouldn't park in the drop-off area, but another, more important lesson: listen to my daughter when she is clearly right.

Thankfully, after she got home that day, we had a very long talk and aired everything . . . and I mean *every* little thing out in the open, no holds barred. As a result, we've grown even closer and our relationship has changed for the better.

The other lesson, which I'm still working on, is that I need to learn to be more selfish. This is a tough one because of the obvious issue of being a parent, and by default, when you are a parent, it's almost impossible to think in those terms. But I'm learning.

The first course of business was asking Josie how she wanted to spend the holidays. It was with a very careful and wary voice that she asked me if it would be okay to spend some time with her dad and his family. At first, I can't lie, it hurt . . . but I got over it because I could see that it was something she really wanted.

So after a long telephone conversation with Matthew, which surprisingly went really well, I agreed to let him stop by in the afternoon on Christmas Day. In addition to that, I agreed to his request to allow Josie to spend a couple of nights with his family to ring in the new year together, making this the first one we've ever been apart.

When she packed up her bag to spend the next two nights at his house, she was so excited. But by the time he came to pick her up a couple of hours ago, her face had fallen. My daughter was worried about me, and the toughest part about this realization was having to tell her that I would be fine . . . and I will . . . I am.

I'm not fine. Not one bit. I feel like climbing the walls.

It's not because of Josie being gone . . . well, maybe just a little bit.

It has more to do with being alone. As in *alone* alone, without a significant other around to share my life. Because in the back of my mind, I know there is someone out there for me who I completely blew it with. And if I have an ounce of the courage that my own daughter had in facing one of the biggest challenges in her life when she met her father, then I should be able to do something about this.

With midnight quickly approaching, I pace back and forth in my living room while *Dick Clark's New Year's Rockin' Eve* is on mute in the background. Honestly, the show kind of sucks since Mr. Clark kicked the bucket and went to that big American Bandstand in the sky, so why I bother to still put it on every year is beyond my comprehension at this point.

Then the plan hits me out of nowhere. It's a crazy one, but whatever, I'm just going to go with it. New year, new me, and a new plan. Because for some reason, it is suddenly of the utmost importance that *this* year be the year I kiss someone at midnight.

And not a relative. And not on the cheek.

I want a full-on slow and sensual, hot and sweet, rough and gentle kiss at midnight from the one man who I know can deliver: Cameron.

Without another minute to spare and giving myself no time to change my mind, I mentally hit the clock on the twenty seconds of utter bravery again to get my ass out the door and into my car. I may have to reset it a few times before I get to Cameron's house, but that's okay too.

I drive like a bat out of hell down my street, blasting the satellite random-mix radio station and singing along as it plays AC/DC's "Back in Black," getting myself all pumped up. Then the song switches over to "All Cried Out" by Lisa Lisa & Cult Jam. I'm singing along at the top of my lungs for the first few bars until I stop because it dawns on me that the words are so freaking depressing. My God, are they depressing and *sooo* not the right thing to be listening to right now. So I turn the radio off.

It's just as well, since I'm about five minutes away from Cameron's house anyway.

This time I don't pull over, I don't hesitate, I don't stop anywhere but in his driveway and put the car in park. Taking a deep and cleansing breath, I hit the reset button on my twenty seconds of insane courage and step outside into the breezy and slightly cool

Miami night and slam my car door shut with way too much enthusiasm, only to remember there is a fatal flaw in my plan.

I didn't account for Cameron not being home.

His car isn't in the driveway, and as the realization hits me, my heart sinks and the wind in my sails is completely gone . . . just like a snap of my fingers.

I don't cry often, if ever, really. Maybe once or twice a year . . . three, tops. I'm a little bit of a freak that way. That's not to say that I don't let things get to me, and I may get a little emotional from time to time.

But with this development . . . it's like a dam breaks inside of me that I can't control.

I lean back against my car door and let the tears loose that have been lying in wait underneath the surface. It's a full-body, racking sob that is so heavy it's quiet. That's how I know it's going to be bad and a long, long cry.

I feel so defeated and wish that I would have come sooner instead of waiting all these stupid weeks to get back here to his door. But it's not meant to be, I guess. I have to accept that and move on.

You're an idiot, I think to myself. Then, through my sniffles and wiping my eyes, I say out loud, "Or you can just come back here when he's home."

"Or you can stay," Cameron's voice says from somewhere behind me. "I prefer the latter, if you want my opinion."

He scares me so much that I yelp out loud and nearly jump out of my own skin.

I ask him in complete shock, "What are you doing here?"

"I live here." I can see the hint of a smile on his face in the darkness. He slowly takes a step or two closer to where I am, then stops a foot away. "The better question is, what are you doing here?"

"It's a long story."

"Is it?" He pulls his phone out of his jeans pocket and then says, "I've got plenty of time."

"What time is it?" I ask.

"Two minutes to midnight."

I comb my fingers through my messy hair, which I'm just now realizing that I didn't even bother to brush. Then I look down at myself; I'm wearing a pair of duck print baby blue pajama bottoms with a white tank top and a gray cotton cardigan that has holes in the pockets, since I've had it for years.

"Okay, two minutes . . . I can do this in two minutes."

"What is it you can do in two minutes, exactly?" he asks, chuckling at me.

"This . . . Cameron, I'm sorry. You were right and I made a stupid mistake. I have been miserable and have missed being with you and spending time with you and getting to know you better. I have been putting myself through hell for no reason other than I was afraid to let myself feel more with you than I ever have before, and I don't want to live like that anymore. I want to be able to wake up next to you—obviously, when I can . . . you know, for now, or however this shakes out, that's not really important—anyway, I want to wake up next to you after having slept in your arms all night. I want to be able to make love to you as often as I want and not feel guilty about the time I spend with you away from my family . . . really, Josie, but that's another story that I don't have time for if I want to make this fit into two minutes. Where was I . . . ? Oh, right! I want to see every single one of your geeky T-shirts that make me smile and make you look insufferably cute . . . and sexy, by the way. I want to draw every single aircraft and spaceship ever created by George Lucas for you so you can hang them up on your walls." I take a quick gulp of air before I pass out from loss of breath from talking too fast. "And last but certainly not least, I want to be able to start over with you and fall in love with you if you'll forgive me for being an idiot, of course."

Cameron stares at me without saying a single word, with precious time running out on the clock.

"What time is it?" I ask and almost leap the last bit of space between us so that I'm a breath away from him. "I need to know what time it is."

Cameron takes his phone out of his pocket and looks at the screen. Grinning, he turns it around so I can see that it's one minute to midnight, then puts it away again.

"Yes! I made it!"

As if a domino effect is taking place, the neighbors on his block, one by one, start to cheer and count as they also prepare for the ball to drop in less than a minute. But he still hasn't said a word. And it occurs to me that perhaps he doesn't want any of it . . . or me. And this was all a waste of time.

"Oh my God, I'm so sorry, Cameron," I say, slightly embarrassed, and take a step back. "I thought that you would be okay with this, that you wanted to start over. I guess . . . I guess I didn't account for this happening in my plan. I'll just go home and—"

"Vanessa, shut up, because you're right, I don't want to start over."

"I'm—"

He puts his finger to my mouth to keep me from talking. "I wasn't finished and we have maybe five, ten seconds tops now, so let me talk."

I nod underneath his finger, but he doesn't take it away. He was right too, because now all around us I can hear his neighbors yelling out: "*Five, four, three, two, one!*"

He wraps his hands around my waist, pulling me flush against his body. Then his one hand skims up my back and around the front until he's cupping my face. Leaning forward another inch, he brushes his lips against mine, but he doesn't kiss me. He whispers, "I don't want to start over . . . I want to pick up where we left off."

Then he kisses me . . . and it's perfect: slow and sensual, hot and sweet, rough and gentle. Just as I imagined it would be.

Cameron pulls back, his dark eyes looking straight into mine, with no hint of hesitation and nothing other than complete adoration in them for me. And with the corners of his lips curling into a genuine smile, he says two more things to me before bringing me inside his house to really celebrate.

"Happy New Year, Vanessa. You had me at George Lucas."

EPILOGUE

Myy mom is the most amazing person I know. When she asked me to be her maid of honor a while ago, I was the one who was honored.

The only problem is that I don't really like speaking in public, so I'll keep this short and sweet and to the point.

It's been my mom and me for a very long time; just the two of us. Then Mr. Thomas came along . . . oops, sorry! I still have a hard time saying Cameron, *or* stepdad.

Anyway, *Cameron* came into our lives and changed everything . . . for the better. Especially for my mom. The one thing more than anything that I've noticed is how they always bring out the best in each other and how they're always finding ways to be cute together when they think nobody is paying attention.

Well, I've got news for you two: I've been paying attention.

And the thing I've taken away from all of the cute stuff and how they are with each other is that they are so in love and perfect for each other, and I only hope that one day I'll find someone who treats me as good as Cameron does my mom.

Until then, I want everyone to raise their glasses to toast to the new couple . . . and yes, Mom, this is only sparkling cider, so don't worry.

To Mr. and Mrs. Cameron Thomas . . . but especially to my mom, who I hope to be like when I grow up, because she is a force to be reckoned with."

ACKNOWLEDGMENTS

This book was written mostly during one of the most stressful times in my life, so like Josie's little short but sweet speech at the very end of the book, I'd like to give a special thank-you to a few people:

My editor at Montlake Romance, Maria Gomez . . . thank you for believing in me, for getting my humor and style of writing, and for being so understanding when I needed you to be.

Jessica Poore, author relations person extraordinaire at Montlake Romance . . . thank you for always responding to any little thing I ever ask of you and for being my kind of people because you love J. J. Abrams and Benedict Cumberbatch.

Melody Guy, who I've now had the pleasure of working with twice and hopefully will again sooner than later. Thank you so much for all the time and effort you devote to my words and making sure they're the best they can be.

To my closest friends and in no particular order: Claire Contreras, Sara Queen, Stephanie Brown, Dionne Simmons, Victoria Carballo, Mirelle Abraham, and finally, Lisa Chamberlin. All of you continue to be there for me in more ways than I can ever dream of, so I thank you for allowing me the honor of calling each of you friend.

To my little people, Belinda and Christian . . . thank you for being MY little people, and I love you both to the moon and back and then back and then back again and again . . .

And finally to MY Cameron, Tyler, and Alex all rolled into one: Kyle . . . "thank you" will never be enough, but I'll say it anyway . . . thank you, baby, and I love you, always.

ABOUT THE AUTHOR

Barbie Bohrman was born and raised in Miami, Florida, and ultimately moved to the Garden State, where she currently resides with her two children and husband. When she is not writing, you can find her trying to get through the 1000+ books on her Kindle, or watching *Lost* or *Seinfeld*.

Connect with the author at:

Facebook:
https://www.facebook.com/pages/Barbie-Bohrman-Author/170019943145037?ref=hl

Goodreads:
https://www.goodreads.com/bbohrman1

Twitter:
@barbie_bohrman

Website/Blog:
www.barbiebohrmanbooks.com